MURMUR

R.E.M.

Other titles in Schirmer's *Classic Rock Albums* series

LET IT BE / ABBEY ROAD
THE BEATLES
Peter Doggett

NEVER MIND THE BOLLOCKS, HERE'S THE SEX PISTOLS
THE SEX PISTOLS
Clinton Heylin

DISRAELI GEARS
CREAM
John Platt

THE RISE AND FALL OF ZIGGY STARDUST AND THE SPIDERS FROM MARS
DAVID BOWIE
Mark Paytress

MEATY, BEATY, BIG AND BOUNCY
THE WHO
John Perry

NEVERMIND
NIRVANA
Jim Berkenstadt and Charles R. Cross

EXILE ON MAIN ST.
THE ROLLING STONES
John Perry

CLASSIC ROCK ALBUMS
Series Editor: Clinton Heylin

MURMUR

R.E.M.

John A. Platt

SCHIRMER BOOKS
An Imprint of Macmillan Library Reference USA
New York

SCHIRMER BOOKS
An Imprint of Macmillan Library Reference USA
1633 Broadway
New York, NY 10019

Library of Congress Catalog Card Number: 99-042127

Printed in the United States of America

Printing number
12345678910

Library of Congress Cataloging-in-Publication Data

Platt, John A.
  Murmur : R.E.M. / John Platt
    p.   cm. – (Classic rock albums)
  Discography: p.
  Includes indexes.
  ISBN 0-02-865062-X (alk. paper)
  1. R.E.M. (Musical group). 2. Rock music—United States—History and criticism. I. Title. II. Series.
ML421.R46P6 1999
782.42166'092'2 21—dc21   99-042127

CONTENTS

CONTENTS

ACKNOWLEDGMENTS

Thanks are again due to noted British R.E.M. archivist and scholar, Tim Abbott. Apart from supplying his usual tapes and cuttings, his input on R.E.M. history was invaluable. Thanks are also due to the following: Jon Storey, Mitch Easter, Marcus Gray, Bob Strano, and Mitch Blank. Extra special thanks to the staff of the Magnolia bakery/café of Bleecker Street, Greenwich Village, NYC. Their apple muffins, black coffee, and conversation each morning enabled the author to face another day at the computer. The usual thanks to Pete Frame, even though he didn't help on this one. Genuine thanks to Richard Carlin at Schirmer Books. Long may his struggle against the Tuning Fork Syndrome continue. And thanks, as well, to his colleague Richard Kassell. Keep sending the wacky e-mails, Richard.

Lastly, I want to express my love and gratitude to my wife, Marylou. After five years she's still trying to explain to me the intricacies of American (as opposed to British) punctuation.

INTRODUCTION

When I first met R.E.M. in December 1983, my impression was of four young guys clearly part of the post (even post-post) Punk Generation. By contrast I saw myself as someone who'd come of age during the '60s and who'd later witnessed, and had a considerable fondness for, punk and its offshoots. By the early '80s I was feeling almost paternal toward any new band playing original music with a distinct '60s influence; and so it was with R.E.M.

The curious thing I was to discover later was that one member of the band (Peter Buck) was a mere four years younger than I and two of the others only six years younger. I remember being slightly shocked by this. It wasn't that, in the time-honored manner of pop groups, they had lied to the press about their ages and were masquerading as teenagers, it was simply an example of the fact that, as with their music, there was considerably more to R.E.M. than met the eye. If nothing else, it helped to explain the maturity shown on *Murmur,* which in many ways seemed slightly at odds with the band's youthful exuberance on-stage and (Michael Stipe somewhat excepted) their largely justified image as party animals off-stage.

That observation will not be explored in depth because this book is not a biography of R.E.M. What it will do is trace in detail the early recording career of one of the most original and musically satisfying bands of the last twenty years—up to and including their groundbreaking first album, *Murmur.* It's a story involving colorful characters, record company politics, misplaced trust and bad business decisions, counterbalanced by faith, integrity, and refusal to compromise.

Michael Stipe, UGA Campus, 1979.
(PHOTO BY TERRY ALLEN)

1

Although the songs on *Murmur* represent the core of the book, all of the songs composed between the band's formation, or shortly thereafter, and the recording of the album, I consider, by extension, to be *Murmur* songs. Partly this is because several songs on the album date from their earliest days and partly because virtually all of their songs, from mid-1980 through late 1982, are of a piece. This is not to say they are all similar in style or content, but simply that any of the songs from that period could have ended up on *Murmur* and not been out of place. Therefore, a discussion and analysis of all of the relevant songs, and not just those that appear on the album, form the other significant section of this book.

It is hoped that this discussion will shed some new light, not only on the songs themselves, but also on the band members, especially on the most enigmatic member, Michael Stipe.

CHRONOLOGY

December 6	Peter Lawrence Buck born Oakland, CA.	1956
July 31	William Thomas Berry born Duluth, MN.	1958
December 17	Michael Edward Mills born Orange County, CA. The Mills family moves to Macon, GA, shortly afterward.	
December 4	John Michael Stipe born Decatur, GA. The family moves frequently owing to Stipe senior's military career.	1960
	Stipe family in Germany.	1967 or 1968
	Buck family moves to Atlanta, GA.	1970
	Berry family moves to Macon, GA. Bill Berry meets Mike Mills at high school shortly thereafter. After an initial period of hating each other, they discover a shared interest in music, resulting in their playing together in various bands throughout high school.	1972
	Stipe family settles in Collinsville, near East St. Louis, IL.	1973
	Bill lands a job as errand boy at the Paragon Music booking agency in Macon.	1976
	Berry meets Ian Copeland, recently arrived from London to work at the agency. His brother Stewart is the drummer with The Police. His other brother, Miles, manages The Police and later runs IRS Records. Ian Copeland introduces Berry and Mills to records by British punk bands.	1977

1978	Summer	Stipe family (minus Michael) moves to Watkinsville, near Athens, GA. Michael joins them at the end of the year. Around the same time, Berry, Mills, and Ian Copeland form a short-lived punk band in Macon, The Frustrations.
	December	Peter Buck applies for a job at the Decatur branch of Wuxtry Records and is offered a position at one of their two branches in Athens. He accepts and moves to Athens.
		Shortly after, he meets and becomes friends with Michael Stipe, who is a regular customer at Wuxtry's.

1979	January	Tired of their respective lives, Berry and Mills decide to go to college and move to Athens to enroll at the University of Georgia. Michael Stipe enrolls at the university at the same time. Also in January, Stipe joins Gangster, a cover band, as vocalist. He adopts the stage name of Michael Valentine and wears a thirties-style mobster suit onstage. He sings with them for nearly a year. At some point during the year, Buck and Stipe begin writing songs together, usually at Wuxtry's. Buck comes up with the melodies on his guitar. Despite his later claim that he'd never played a guitar before the formation of R.E.M., it is now known that he'd played, albeit in a very rudimentary fashion, for years.
	Summer	Buck and Stipe begin hanging out/rehearsing with Buck's Wuxtry boss, Dan Wall, at Wall's residence, a converted church on Oconee Street in Athens. The proposed band doesn't work out.
	Autumn	When Wall moves out of the church, he sublets it to Buck, Buck's brother Ken, and UGA student/DJ Kathleen O'Brien. Within a month Stipe moves in as well. Buck and Stipe consider the possibilities of forming a serious band.

| 1980 | January | Kathleen O'Brien introduces Buck to Berry and Mills at a party and suggests that they get together for a jam session. Stipe meets them shortly thereafter and, without much enthusiasm on either side, rehearsals are arranged. |
| | March | After a couple of no-shows, the quartet finally get together at the church. Further rehearsals follow. Around the same time Berry and Kathleen O'Brien become an item, and Berry moves into the church. With her birthday coming up, O'Brien cajoles the band into playing at her party. They finally agree. The rehearsal schedule is stepped-up and songs are written. Mills now spends most nights sleeping at the church. |

R.E.M.: <u>MURMUR</u>

April 5 Playing under a hastily-agreed-upon name, Twisted Kites, the new band makes its debut at O'Brien's party. Their repertoire consists of about eighteen songs. Roughly twelve are originals.

April 18 Deciding they need a permanent name, they sit up all night to make the choice. Wisely eschewing such tasteful appellations as Cans of Piss and Slut Bank, they finally come up with R.E.M.

April 19 The newly named band make their first public appearance at The Koffee Klub in Athens. Unfortunately, the police raid the club and close it down shortly after they begin their set. At this show, the band meet Bertis Downs, who subsequently becomes their lawyer.

May 6 R.E.M. play their first completed public show at Tyrone's, the club that was to be the group's favorite Athens venue until it burned down in January 1982.

June 6 The band is videotaped at a practice session at the Decatur branch of Wuxtry's. Part of the soundtrack eventually becomes the first R.E.M. bootleg.

End of June "Gardening at Night," described by the band as their "first real song," is written on the porch of the church one morning after a party. Shortly afterward, the members of the band, Kathleen O'Brien, and the other church residents, move out. In due course it becomes derelict and in 1990 all but the steeple is demolished.

July 18/19 R.E.M. play their first out-of-state shows in Carrboro, NC. The shows are booked by record store owner Jefferson Holt. In the late summer Holt moves to Athens and in due course becomes R.E.M.'s manager.

February 8 R.E.M.'s first proper recording session takes place at Bombay Studios, Smyrna, GA.

1981

April 15 The band's first visit to producer Mitch Easter's Drive-In Studios, Winston-Salem, NC. They record the tracks that are subsequently used for their promo cassette and first single.

July R.E.M.'s first single "Radio Free Europe/Sitting Still" released on Hib-Tone Records.

October 2–4 and 7 The band return to Drive-In Studios to cut tracks for a proposed EP.

January 27–28 Further sessions at Drive-In for the EP.

February 1–2 and 8 The band record a demo tape for RCA Records, at RCA's studios in New York.

May 31 R.E.M. sign with IRS Records.

June 1 Final EP session at Drive-In.

August 24 R.E.M.'s *Chronic Town* EP released on IRS.

December At a studio in Atlanta, the band work with Stephen Hague, a possible producer for their first album. The results are a disaster.

Early January At the request of the band, Mitch Easter is brought back as producer, but IRS insists on a test recording in a 24-track studio. Easter chooses Reflection Studios in Charlotte, NC. The band like the result, but IRS doesn't. R.E.M. hold firm and are allowed to make the album with Easter.

January 20–February 23 Reflection Studios, Charlotte, NC, *Murmur* recording sessions.

April 13 *Murmur* album and a single, "Radio Free Europe" (rerecorded version), issued by IRS.

ONE
CHRONIC ATTEMPTS: R.E.M.'S FIRST SONGS

When R.E.M. formed in March 1980, none of the members wanted to be part of a cover band. For drummer Bill Berry and bassist Mike Mills the reason was simple: They had done that already. By contrast, Peter Buck's motivation was more pragmatic. As he told me in 1983,

> When the band started, no one was really sure what instrument I was going to play. Mike could play the guitar better than me, and I knew I wasn't going to play the drums. It was suggested that I play the bass, but I could never work it out, so in the end I became the guitar player. I couldn't learn the simplest songs, "Gloria" was about all I could manage—three chords and a cloud of dust. So we started writing our own.

In fact, even before the band's inception they had each written songs, even if, in the case of Buck and singer Michael Stipe, it had only been for a few months. No one knows for sure how many of these pre-R.E.M. efforts made it into the new band's set list, and the only ones that can be positively assigned to a time before the quartet's formation are "Action" and "Narrator."

"Action" dates from Berry and Mills's period with the Frustrations, the short-lived punk band they formed with Ian Copeland, in Macon, in 1978. That "Action" survived into R.E.M.'s repertoire suggests that it was the best of whatever Mills/Berry originals the Frustrations performed. This survival says little for the other songs (assuming there were any) since "Action" is, by any standards, pretty dreadful. Although it remained in R.E.M.'s set list for at least the remainder of 1980, "Action" was one of the first originals they dropped and it was never recorded by them.

Other than the fact that "Narrator" predates R.E.M. and was written by Bill alone, nothing is known about its origins. In all respects it's a bet-

R.E.M.: <u>MURMUR</u>

ter song than "Action," but that's not saying much. What it sounds like is an early '60s novelty song, although "Narrator," unlike "Action" has an engaging melody and even a simple story line. It's the saga of a young boy watching underwater explorer Jacques Cousteau on television in 1972. He decides that he wants to be the show's eponymous hero and, hence, its narrator. The payoff comes at the end when we discover that the young lad in the song can't swim—something of a hindrance in a show about underwater exploration. Judging by the few extant performance tapes, R.E.M. obviously enjoyed playing it. Unfortunately, they can't get around the fact that it's, well . . . silly. Although later revived and recorded by the R.E.M. offshoot band, Hindu Love Gods, R.E.M. realized that "Narrator" didn't fit their image and subsequently dropped it.

Much the same may be said of virtually all the band's original songs written before the summer of 1980. Over the years, indeed as far back as late 1983, Buck has suggested that there were as many as sixty of these early efforts. "Some were OK, some were horrible. We wrote about three a week. Loads of songs, thank God, the world will never hear."

Because tapes of the band remain scarce for the whole of 1980, it's hard to disprove Buck's numbers. Most observers agree, however, that sixty is probably a gross overestimate of their output. Even half that number is probably excessive. Despite Peter's understandable wish that the world should never hear any of them, some twelve songs (aside from "Action" and "Narrator") from their formative period circulate among collectors. Even though many songs are lost forever, those that do exist provide a sufficient body of work to assess the musical outpourings—and to some extent the mindset—of the band in its earliest phase.

Of the twelve songs, six were certainly written prior to June 1980: "Dangerous Times," "All the Right Friends," "Mystery to Me," "Different Girl," "Baby I," and "Permanent Vacation." Dating is possible since they all appear on the infamous "Wuxtry" tape recorded on June 6, 1980 (see Chapter 3). The other songs, "Body Count," "Smalltown Girl," "Scherherazade," and "Lisa Says," make their earliest known appearance on a tape recorded live at Tyrone's in Athens, Georgia, on October 4, 1980, and, therefore, could have been written at any time prior to that day. Stylistically, however, they are so similar to the earliest songs, that they, too, in all likelihood, date from before the summer.

The remaining songs, "Wait" and "That Beat," don't appear on tapes until early 1981; so conceivably, they weren't written until then. If that is the case, they represent an almost aberrant return to the style of the earliest songs. Because that seems unlikely, and unless some hard evidence is presented, I'll stick with the idea that they are also part of the original batch of songs written before the watershed "Gardening at Night."

As anyone who has heard these songs will testify, they are almost uniformly inept. They also bear little relation to what are usually considered early R.E.M. songs, i.e., the ones that appear on *Chronic Town* and *Murmur.* They have been described as "pop songs," "punk thrash," and more commonly as attempts at a '60s garage band sound—all of which have a certain validity. Also true is that they are charming and enthusiastic, to which one could also add naive and avowedly adolescent. Tony Fletcher, in his biography of R.E.M., *Remarks*, suggests that an album of these early songs, recorded live, would have been a "fine manic pop record." This is an understandable point of view, but one undoubtedly affected by hindsight. The reality, I'm afraid, is that, with one or two exceptions, these songs are of historical interest only. The band obviously thought so too, because in live performance, most were replaced as soon as they'd written something better.

One aspect of these songs is worthy of some investigation: the lyrics. Most of Stipe's earliest lyrics are, in common with the music they accompany, enthusiastic, naive, and very simple, and they cover a narrow range of subjects like dating, partying, and boredom. The one exception is "Body Count," which seems to be about a Vietnam vet (Stipe's father?). Unfortunately, the song is saddled with one of their least memorable melodies, even for this era.

Stipe has stated that it took him several years to gain the confidence to write a song in the first person. None of the records, up to and including *Reckoning*, their second album, contain such songs. Therefore, if you've only heard the records and none of the early tapes, his statement can be taken at face value. Interestingly, however, most of his pre-"Gardening at Night" songs *are* written in the first person. More significantly, perhaps, since coming out in the early '90s, Stipe has claimed (most recently on VH1's *Behind the Music* documentary) that he never wrote gender-specific songs. Once again he seems to have forgotten his earliest lyrics, the majority of which are about girls—two even have the

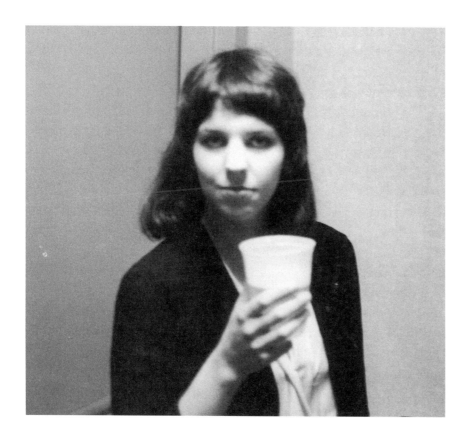

Kathleen O'Brien.
(PHOTO BY SANDRA LEE-
PHIPPS)

word "girl" in the title. While there are a number of reasons why any artist might want to forget his earliest work, in Stipe's case, one reason would seem to be that it doesn't jive with, as he put it to *Face* in 1995, his fondness for "gender-fucking stuff."

Related to the gender issue, too, is the surprising misogyny of several early lyrics. The girls in Stipe's early songs lie, cheat, frustrate, and, on occasion, should be considered dangerous. They are referred to, pejoratively, as "baby" and "sugar." If this isn't blatant enough, Stipe could really get into it while improvising on stage. At the end of one performance of "All the Right Friends," he declaims, "Baby, let's face it, you're all washed up. I said, darling, there's only one place for you, and that's the graveyard with the other corpses." Even more extreme is his spoken addition to a live version of the Velvet Underground's famously unsubtle "There She Goes Again." Stipe's extemporization, delivered with unsavory passion, goes: "She's down on her two knees / She's pulling down your pants / You'd better hit her."

So what's going on here? As far as I know, Marcus Gray, in *It Crawled from the South*, is the only writer, to date, to address the issue of the misogyny in these songs. If nothing else, he rightly points out that, "This is not the gentle, sensitive and evolved Michael Stipe of popular myth, the one his followers have come, if not to know, then certainly to obsess about." Gray goes on to argue that the misogyny is so blatant and obnoxious that it must be a joke, albeit one in bad taste. He further suggests that if you went to an early R.E.M. gig, you were there to party and, in his view, unless you were sober, overly politically sensitive, and/or possessed acute hearing, you would simply not have taken stock of, let alone been offended by, the lyrics.

While there may be an element of truth to his arguments, the all-pervasive nature of the misogyny suggests something deeper than a joke. How then can one reconcile this apparent anger at women, as exemplified in these songs, with the "evolved" and "sensitive" Stipe? One crass and unlikely explanation would be that he simply disliked women, until he grew up and discovered that, as a group, women are no better or worse than men.

A more complex explanation would involve Michael's other famous comment after coming out: that he had always been completely comfortable with his bisexuality. In the real world, few young people are totally at ease with their sexuality—even when it conforms to society's norms; most suffer from some degree of anxiety and inadequacy. If your preferences run counter to those norms—and bisexuality certainly does that—anxiety and stress are probably increased. Maybe Stipe was lucky and was always comfortable with his sexuality. Even so, he must have been aware that not everybody else would be. It's a classic behavioral pattern for people in their teens and early twenties to try to fit in with their peer group, even if it runs contrary to their natural inclinations. They will even exaggerate what they think of as "normal behavior" to gain acceptance. If that is what Stipe was attempting (possibly subconsciously), then how better to convince people you're "normal" than by putting down women—because, after all, that's what "real" (if stereotypical) men do. And where better to display these bogus sentiments than in song lyrics?

In the absence of statements on the subject from Stipe or those who knew him at the time, it is impossible to verify this theory, either in relation to the lyrics or to how his sexual preferences were viewed by his peer group, or wider society, in Athens. Ultimately, therefore, the motivation that lay behind Stipe's early lyrics is doomed to remain an enigma. In some ways those early lyrics are more mysterious than the most cryptic ones on *Murmur*, because they seem totally unlike the perceived image of Stipe; whereas, for all their obtuseness, the *Murmur* lyrics seem completely characteristic of their writer.

Whatever interest lies in analyzing Stipe's earliest lyrics, those lyrics and their music remain nothing more than juvenilia, and it's hardly surprising that R.E.M. wanted to come up with better material. More specifically, it seems that Mike Mills, in particular, felt that their early material presented little challenge musically, and began pushing for the band to write more complex material—especially as Buck was rapidly improving as a guitarist. Almost as if to prove the point, he brought in "(Don't Go Back to) Rockville" in June 1980.

Although credited to all four members, it subsequently emerged that Mike was "Rockville"'s sole composer. As Buck later said, "I think I put a riff in, and Michael changed the bridge or something." Other than that, it was all Mike's, including the lyrics. In its original form as a fast rocker, "Rockville" is superficially similar to the band's first songs. In every other respect, however, it is a far more sophisticated piece of work. The melody is distinctive, the hook line is memorable, and, instrumentally, all three players sound as though they are stretching themselves. The lyrics, almost for the first time with R.E.M., are integrated with the music, as opposed to being an ill-fitting afterthought.

While by no stretch of the imagination could they be described as deep or poetic, the lyrics of "Rockville" are well thought out, imaginative, and tell an easily understood story. It's a simple plea to an unnamed girl, who, unhappy with her life, is planning to return to her dismal hometown. The singer is trying to convince her that she will not only be missed, but more importantly she will "wind up in some factory," miserable. The girl in question was, in fact, Ingrid Schorr, a friend of the band's, who rehearsed with, but quickly left, Stipe's sister's group Oh-ok. The "Rockville" in the song is Rockville, Maryland, which, as Bill Berry later remarked, is "a real factory town, not anywhere you'd want to visit."

"Rockville," remained in the act for eighteen months or so, but was ultimately dropped, only to be revived during the *Reckoning* sessions in December 1983. The original intention was to cut the song as a birthday

gift for their lawyer and friend Bertis Downs. Shortly after the recording Bill Berry commented, "We thought, 'let's give it a real country twang,' and it came out really good. So we added a few parts to it, like the piano and the screeching tremolo guitar. We thought it was good, but even then we almost didn't put it on the album, as we thought it wasn't really representative of us. But then we thought, 'What the hell,' so we did." It was this new version (minus the piano) that became a live staple for several years.

Berry is correct in suggesting that "Rockville" did not represent the band. Although he was talking about the new countrified version of the song, it is arguably true of the original as well. However, it is tempting to speculate on what might have happened back in the summer of 1980, when Mills wrote the song, if things had gone differently. "Rockville" is a superior pop song, and as such, a more logical development from the earliest R.E.M. originals than the more esoteric material that did emerge. If Stipe had not blossomed as a lyricist, and if Buck and Berry had pulled back from composing off-the-wall material with Mills, then a band with Mills as the main composer and lyricist of classy, if somewhat straightforward, rock songs is at least conceivable. "Rockville," under those circumstances, might well have become representative of the band. Of course, by either accident or design, they came up with a different approach that was to transform them into one of the most original bands since the 1960s.

Mike Mills wasn't the only member of R.E.M. to demand changes by the summer of 1980. Michael Stipe was becoming increasingly fed up with having to shout lyrics over music that raced by at ever-increasing tempos. In fact, the structure of the early songs virtually precluded singing at all. To compensate, he tried slowing down his delivery, which sometimes forced the others to stop thrashing away—but sometimes didn't. Also, he wanted to write more challenging lyrics. As he said in late '83, "The early songs were all very skeletal and the lyrics were like simple pictures, but after a year I got really bored with that. So I started experimenting with lyrics that didn't make exact linear sense and it's just gone from there." Since the first evidence of this new writing style was "Gardening at Night," which was written toward the end of June 1980, Stipe's remark confirms the fact that he'd been writing songs for several months prior to the formation of the band.

With "Gardening at Night" Stipe was now moving into the era of "lyrics that don't make exact linear sense." So what exactly is he singing about? And not just on "Gardening at Night," but on just about every R.E.M. song for the next four years, including, most certainly, the whole of *Murmur*? Perhaps a more immediate question would be: why write songs that most people (and even, on occasion, Stipe himself) can't understand? A simplistic answer is that he was bored with the way he had been writing, and "Gardening at Night," and the songs that followed, is what came out. Needless to say, there has to be more to it than that.

One obvious fact about Stipe's early "skeletal" lyrics, possible misogyny notwithstanding, is that there is obviously very little of Stipe in them. While he may have been less sensitive and evolved than he later became, Stipe was, nonetheless, an educated young man with an interest in, among other things, literature, film, and art, not to mention mythology and, in some form or another, religion. It was perfectly natural, therefore, that as an aspiring writer he would want his work to reflect those interests. The songs prior to "Gardening at Night" do not. But with that song and those that followed, images drawn from, or reflective of, those topics crop up in Stipe's songs.

Also, it would be almost unheard of for a young writer not to inject something of his own life into his work. Thus, despite the self-imposed restriction that he was not going to write in the first person, aspects of Stipe's life and preoccupations do crop up in most of the lyrics starting with "Gardening at Night." You have to look pretty closely to find them, though. As Stipe has said, "I'm not about to split myself open, to gut myself onstage and spill myself all over people. Number one, because there's not much inside that people ought to see, and number two, I don't want to put myself in the position where my ribcage is split open to people I don't know." On the surface it's a reasonable position to have taken. It's *his* life, after all, and, if nothing else, it placed him a million miles from the confessional songwriters of the early seventies like Jackson Browne, whose entire lives were an open book. Nonetheless, methinks the boy doth protest just a little too much.

The question remains, though: why did his lyrics have to be so obscure? After all, even the most poetic of rock lyricists usually find ways of making their images and metaphors concrete enough to get their intentions and meanings across.

In general terms a plausible, if mildly cryptic, answer was provided by Peter Buck when he told R.E.M. biographer Tony Fletcher, "Part of it is that as we went along we realized that we didn't want to be a straight narrative band that has stories in our songs that began and ended. You can put meaning in there—you can write a song about something without ever really referring to what you're writing about—by using evocative phrases, by association of words that you wouldn't normally associate, by the power of the music itself and the melodies. You can get the feeling from that experience without ever actually referring to the experience itself." Or, as he told *Rolling Stone* in 1983, "We never wanted to spell things out. If you want that, go and listen to The Clash. They're a newspaper and we're not."

Buck's comments answer the question of the enigmatic lyrics, but only up to a point. One is left wondering whether Michael really wanted to be heard, both in a psychological sense and in an artistic one. Most writers want their work to be understood, and at times, Stipe has expressed frustration when listeners don't completely understand a song that he thought was crystal clear. This has most often been in reference to his later lyrics, which seem less obtuse than the earlier ones. Even so, his attitude to pre-1984 material has frequently been ambiguous. For example, in 1988 he told a *New Musical Express* interviewer that most of the lyrics of *Murmur* were "right there." Likewise, if asked, he has often discussed the meanings of individual songs and lines, even if his answers are often as impenetrable as the original lyrics. Conversely he has frequently given stock "well, it means whatever you think it means" answers, and, on occasion, claimed that the meanings of certain songs, *Murmur*'s "Pilgrimage," for example, were as much a mystery to him as to anybody else.

There is another, very literal, sense in which one may wonder whether Stipe wanted to be heard. From R.E.M.'s earliest days, listeners complained that it was tough simply deciphering what he was singing, let alone what the lyrics meant. One waggish critic even went so far as to refer to *Murmur* as "Mumbles." Stipe was always quick to defend his sound, as in 1983, when he stated, "It's just the way I sing. If I tried to control it, it would be pretty false." While his engaging nasal whine and loose approach to enunciation has always been a problem to some degree, there is no doubt that from about 1985 the problem lessened. Around the same time, strangely enough, his lyrics begin to make more literal sense.

So what is one to make of Stipe and his frequently inaudible and often enigmatic lyrics, at least during the period from the summer of 1980, when "Gardening at Night" emerged, through the beginning of 1983, when *Murmur* was recorded? One possibility is that, lacking confidence in his writing skills, he hid behind obfuscation, both in terms of his lyrics and their delivery. While I certainly don't believe that, I think there is a distinct possibility that he was genuinely afraid of revealing too much of himself through his work. His stance may have at times seemed coy—hiding behind a veil of mystery, while at the same time dropping hints as to the meaning of his lyrics—but I've always thought that his diffidence was genuine. Maybe all one can say, in the end, is that he was (and probably remains) a genuinely self-effacing person who, at the same time, wants to be heard—by no means an unusual combination of traits in those of an artistic disposition.

Although it's quite acceptable to consider the person when considering their art—art, after all, is a highly personal business—the important thing is the end result, in this case Stipe's lyrics and R.E.M.'s music. In this respect I find Stipe's lyrics fascinating in themselves, but more importantly, it was their blending with the music in unique and original ways, that, among other factors, made the R.E.M. of the early '80s such an extraordinary and important band. In this respect I totally agree with Peter Buck: you can often achieve a greater effect by implication, rather than by being literal or prosaic. As he said, "You have to short-circuit the whole idea that literal language is what things are, because literal language is just code for what happens."

We are still left, however, with the original question: what is Stipe singing about and, for that matter, should we try and find out? One school of thought suggests that you shouldn't bother. You can't hear the words most of the time and, even when you can, you have Stipe's own admission that his early '80s lyrics do not make linear sense. What is important is what the words mean to you, the listener, along with the mood created by the voice itself and its interplay with the music.

Balanced against that is not only Stipe's belief, some of the time at least, that most of the songs are about something, but also clues given by him, and the others, regarding specific inspirations and meanings. In one sense, just by making these comments, Stipe is validating an interpretive approach to his work. More fundamentally, it can be argued that it is to everyone's benefit when light is thrown upon any work, offering another way to see it.

Difficulties abound, of course, in interpreting Stipe's lyrics. Two difficulties have already been mentioned: the lack of linear sense and the sheer inaudibility of many of the words. Beyond that, Stipe occasionally leaves out essential parts of speech and/or makes use of words or phrases purely for their sound.

Then there is his use of "random" words and juxtapositions. In my interview with Stipe in 1983, he denied using the William Burroughs/Brion Gysin "cut-up method," where words or sentences are cut from existing pieces of text and fitted together in a random fashion. Stipe told me that he found the method "interesting," but that he didn't use it because "it leaves too much to chance, and if you've only got four minutes to get an idea across you can't really use chance that much. So my lyrics are not stream of consciousness or cut-up at all." By contrast another band member told me that when stumped for a lyric, Michael would write down phrases on pieces of paper, throw them into a hat, and pull them out at random. He would then use the results just as they came out. What Stipe *did* admit was writing down odd or unusual things he'd overheard and then using them more or less verbatim in a lyric. Not quite as random as some of his other methods, but certainly not designed to aid meaning.

All of these factors militate against successfully interpreting any Stipe song from top to bottom. Nonetheless, with the clues dropped over the years as a starting point, coupled with a reasonable interpretive faculty and a fondness for detective work, it is possible to find meaning in virtually every Stipe song.

Consequently, I have attempted to give an interpretation of every known R.E.M. song from "Gardening at Night," composed, as noted, in June 1980, through "Talking About the Passion," written just in time for the *Murmur* sessions in January 1983. This amounts to some 28 songs: the five that appeared on *Chronic Town*, the twelve on *Murmur*, two that weren't recorded until *Reckoning*, two that finally showed up on *Lifes Rich Pageant* (one admittedly with new words and title), four that appeared on B-sides and/or compilations, plus three that remain unreleased. They are arranged roughly in the order in which they were composed or—at least—when they first appeared in the act, which in most cases is probably the same. In each instance there is an assessment of the music as well.

Very early on, the band decided that it was so rare for one person to have written a complete song on their own that it made sense to credit everyone jointly. This had the added benefit that all of them earned exactly the same income on song royalties, thus sidestepping the jealousy that has broken up so many other bands in the past.

R.E.M., on stage at least, featured what appeared to be a perfectly standard line-up of guitar, bass, and drums, plus Michael's vocals. Their maturing approach to songwriting, however, also signaled subtle changes in the way each member tackled his role. In late 1983, Stipe summed up this unique approach: "One part of the band will be doing this very rhythmic thing or melodic type of thing, and then someone else will come in and do something that's the exact opposite. The bass may be carrying the melody, and then the vocal might come in and do something without resonance or melody at all. I'm really pleased with that." In the same interview Buck added that all of the band's members had floating parts. Mike frequently changed his bass lines, Bill could alter his drum parts if he felt like it, and, of course, Michael constantly changed the lyrics. Curiously, Buck himself claimed that his parts were the most stable.

It was this new approach that was first made manifest on "Gardening at Night."

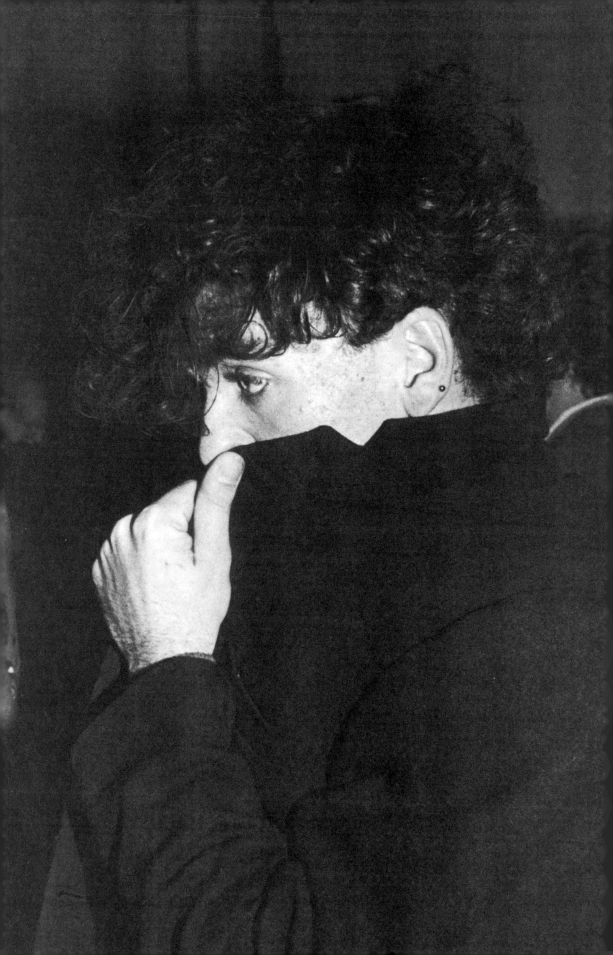

TWO

TALKING ABOUT
THE PASSION:
THE <u>MURMUR</u>-ERA SONGS

With "Gardening at Night," several things happened at once. Primarily a new dramatic quality entered their music. What had previously been weak pastiche was now strong and (despite some obvious '60s influences) highly original. The melody grabs you instantly and yet leaves something more hovering around its edges that demands repeated listening for full appreciation. The playing, even on the earliest known performances, jumps several notches as well; the musicians sound as though their hearts are really in it. And unlike "Rockville," which is tight and compact, the more fluid structure of "Gardening at Night" gives them room for a degree of spontaneity. Because of the way the melody line is written, the same may said about Stipe's vocal; he could effectively weave in and out of the music to subtle and dramatic effect.

While "Gardening at Night" was no doubt heavily rearranged by Mills and Berry, it was initially a Buck/Stipe composition. As Stipe later recalled, "I distinctly remember the afternoon we wrote 'Gardening at Night.' We were sitting out on a mattress on the porch [of the church] and I thought it was the first real song we did."

Buck later claimed that he was influenced by the drop-D tuning that Neil Young had used on "Cinnamon Girl," but for most listeners Buck's ringing 12-string Rickenbacker held echoes of the Byrds. While it's true

"Gardening
at Night"

Early 1980 and Stipe is already trying to avoid the paparazzi.
(Photo by Terry Allen)

21

that any time a guitar player strums an electric 12-string, comparisons to Roger McGuinn (the Byrds' guitarist) inevitably spring to mind; in the case of R.E.M., it was always overstated. And apart from anything else, the comparisons continued well after the time that Buck had effectively forsworn the 12-string in favor of a 6-string Fender.

"Gardening at Night" is one of the rare R.E.M. songs where the inspiration for the lyric is not only known but also undisputed. In late 1983 Peter Buck told me, "There was an old guy in my neighborhood who would be out gardening at 2 A.M., in his suit and tie. I'd see him when I was out trying to get beer at the Magic Market, or somewhere. I told Michael about the guy and he wrote the song."

Of course, knowing that doesn't help much with decoding the song. Stipe, in one of his playful, but less-than-communicative moods, later stated, "Some people think it's about my father, some people think it's about drugs, and some people think it's about gardening at night. It's all of them." Then again, there's Buck's other comment from the same 1983 interview: "It's basically a metaphor for the uselessness of everything. But if you didn't get that, I'm not surprised, it's kind of a confused song." Yes, it is.

The central question is: What is implied by the metaphorical use of the phrase "gardening at night"?—because it's clearly used in more than a literal sense. Generally speaking, any activity normally done in daylight and done instead at night, for no obvious reason, is a symbol of covert activity and pursuant guilt.

Bearing that in mind, it doesn't seem to be too much of a stretch to suggest that what the narrator is describing, in part at least, is the aftermath of a nocturnal tryst. It should be noted that the "I" in poetry and novels is usually regarded as just another character created by the writer. Consequently, Stipe may not be talking about himself. This applies to all his lyrics, even when there is the strongest suspicion that they are auto-biographical.

The first line, "I see your money on the floor, I felt the pocket change," would fit a situation where someone (male or female) has taken their pants off prior to having sex. Loose change has spilled out, and the narrator picks it up afterward.

What we are witnessing, perhaps, is the couple being interrupted or awakened. This is implied by the line, "We ankled up the garbage sound, but they were busy in the rows." Given Stipe's penchant for leaving out vital words, a simple interpolation would render the line, "We ankled up [got up], because of the garbage sound." Quite simply, they were awakened/interrupted by the garbagemen loudly emptying trash cans. And it's no longer night.

The narrator seems less than happy or, at best, confused. Some sort of veil has been lifted and "the sun just hurts my eyes." He is forced to confront those feelings that "just don't seem to be too real" in broad daylight.

One thing that may trouble the narrator is the youth of the person he's been with: "Your sister said that you're too young." Only twice in the song is someone addressed directly as "you"—first, whoever dropped the money and next, the person who is "too young." If the two people addressed are one and the same, then age is most certainly an issue. The second part of that line, "They should know, they've been there twice," though still cryptic, is more easily understood when you know that, in live versions, Stipe frequently changed the line to "She should know, she's been there twice." If the "there" where she's been "twice" is the garden at night with the narrator, the implication is that the sister and the narrator have had sex as well. If it's true, no wonder the narrator is uncomfortable and perhaps confused.

Perhaps as a result of his turmoil, the narrator's gardening at night was fruitless or "just didn't grow," which might refer to anything from erectile dysfunction to a generalized sense of futility—or, to extend the botanical metaphor, the barrenness of the relationship.

While the narrator does not feel remorse ("Somewhere it must be time for penitence [but] gardening at night is never where"), one senses his anguish and a desire to ease it. "Call the prayer line for a change / The charge is changing every month"; and later, "The call was 2 and 51 / They said it couldn't be arranged," undoubtedly refers to a dial-a-prayer service. "Two and 51" could be either the duration of the call (2 minutes and 51 seconds) or the cost (2 dollars and 51 cents). Calling the prayer line is the narrator's attempt to make sense of his feelings.

If nothing else, this word choice is an excellent use of language. "For a change" can mean to do something new to alleviate boredom, or to alter one's life. And "change" here refers to the earlier phrase, "pocket change." There is yet another pun in the line "The charge is changing every month." This can literally refer to money (again) or to the fact that, for the narrator, the emotional cost keeps going up in some way. Viewed in that light, the following line, "They said it couldn't be arranged," could easily refer to the inability of the prayer line people to help the narrator. All of which makes Buck's reading of the song as "a metaphor for the uselessness of everything" a tad more cogent. Think of his comment in terms of the narrator's varied and futile attempts to find comfort and make sense of his situation.

"Gardening at Night" is not great poetry, nor should it be viewed as such. If nothing else, it lacks cohesion and consistency of viewpoint, and it's unnecessarily vague. But as a rock song it really is quite remarkable. And for a young lyricist it's a surprisingly mature work, both in its subject matter, use of language, and evocative images. It's still, as Buck says, "kind of a confused song," but that shouldn't detract from either its overall excellence or the quality of individual lines or choice of words.

"Just a Touch" is usually grouped with the band's earliest material, but only because it appears on the June 6, 1980, Wuxtry tape. However, it was written the same week as "Gardening at Night." While not an equal of the latter, it stands head and shoulders above the Spring 1980 songs and for that reason alone deserves to be singled out from them. Musically, it's the first of the band's out-and-out rockers that doesn't sound like it's being played by a bunch of amateurs thrashing away to no real purpose. There is a genuine and discernible melody in there and the staccato delivery, instrumental and vocal, of the chorus is highly effective.

The verse also contains a structural device that's worthy of note: in each line Stipe sets up a proposition or question on one vocal level ("Well what in the world?) and then drops to little more than a whisper, in order to respond ("Women in black"). Not exactly revolutionary, but it demonstrates that Stipe was now thinking about the form of his words and how they sound when sung. Certainly there are none of the images and metaphors that enrich his best lyrics, but it's a solid, workmanlike job for all that.

Even if you know only the words, it's still quite easy to discern the subject matter of the song: the death of a celebrity and how the individuals named in the song learn of it.

In fact, thanks to an unusually copious explanation from Stipe, a lot more is known about the origins of "Just a Touch" than about almost any of his songs from this era. Apparently it relates to his tenure as a busboy at Sonny & Cher's (just "Sonny's" in the song), a disco in East St. Louis—specifically on August 16, 1977, the day that Elvis Presley died. Apart from the individuals receiving the news, the song also mentions the women in black who turn up to mourn their dead hero. The incredible irony was that the top of the bill that night was an Elvis impersonator named Orion, who, according to Stipe, was completely unaware, until he arrived, that the King had died. Orion's poster allegedly read, "Is it Elvis? Or just a touch?"

"Just a Touch," although a stage favorite, was dropped relatively quickly but briefly revisited during the *Reckoning* sessions. It received a full-scale revival on 1985's *Fables* tour and was subsequently rerecorded and released on *Lifes Rich Pageant*. The mid-'80s version was fundamentally the same as the original, just beefed up somewhat. It did, however, pick up a few new lyrics, including a reference to Tyrone's, their late lamented home-away-from-home in Athens, which had burned down in

Fashion mavens all: Stipe, Jerry Ayers, Lynda Stipe, a friend, and Linda Hopper in a scene from Laura Levine's film *Just Like a Movie*.
(PHOTO BY LAURA LEVINE)

January 1982. There are also a couple of new lines, including, "I can't see, I'm so young, I'm so goddamn young," which was lifted directly from the *Easter* version of "Privilege (Set Me Free)" by Patti Smith.

"Burning Down"/"Ages of You"

It would be gratifying to think that, having written "Gardening at Night," R.E.M. continued onward and upward, composing ever more complex and wonderful songs, as well as immediately ditching all their rotten ones. Needless to say, that's not what happened. Although they would have recognized "Gardening at Night" as their best song to date, it probably took them awhile to realize what a radical departure it represented. In the interim it was inevitable that they would compose a few also-rans.

Such was the case, one assumes, with "Burning Down." Not that it's a poor song by any means. It features a pleasantly quirky melody and a memorable riff, coupled with some intriguing lyrics. It's been suggested that the words foreshadow Stipe's lyrical fascination with the Old South that came to fruition with 1985's *Reconstruction of the Fables*. The references to a burning plantation and to someone whose hands are tied and whose feet are bound are certainly suggestive of the Civil War and perhaps a slave uprising.

More interesting is the appearance in the third verse of "Johnny Mike" who is "reading in the yard." It's too much of a coincidence to believe that (John Michael) Stipe is talking about anybody other than himself. This might, then, make some sense of the first two lines of the opening verse, "From the back of my neck / Wired a glass jaw." A glass jaw, particularly among boxers, refers to a weakness in that area, the implication being that the slightest tap will break it like glass. Is Stipe recalling an incident from his childhood when his jaw, broken in a fight, had to be wired?

Putting the two images together you might have a convalescing young Stipe reading in the yard about the Civil War or possibly the civil rights movement. Unfortunately, the lyrics of "Burning Down" are even more confusing than "Gardening at Night," and trying to make sense of them, without some direction from their author, is ultimately a futile exercise.

The band's standards of what constituted a good song was obviously changing, and within a very short time they realized that "Burning Down" didn't really make it. Rather than scrap it altogether, they rewrote it. As Buck later recalled: "We played it for around a month, [actually somewhat longer than that] and we didn't really like it, but we did like that one little riff. So we kept the riff and rewrote the song and called it 'Ages of You.'"

Knowing that the two are related, it's possible to hear the connection. However, while "Burning Down" is a mid-tempo rocker, "Ages of You," while by no means a ballad, is decidedly slower and has an almost wistful quality. The words of the new song have been criticized as being little more than off-the-cuff nonsense, but in my view that's very unfair. The two verses make almost perfect sense if you view them as observations made by Michael while seated on a train. They are, one suspects, almost literal transcriptions from his infamous notebooks, rendered without any attempts to incorporate the conjunctions usually considered essential to comprehension. The end result is not unlike a haiku.

The title "Ages of You" is probably no more than a poetic way of suggesting someone the writer has known for a long time. And although there's nothing in the lyrics to support it, the overall tone suggests that "You" is someone he's fond of.

Although it's doubtful that either "Burning Down" or "Ages of You" were seriously considered for album release, they were both recorded. While "Ages of You" was cut at the *Murmur* sessions, "Burning Down" wasn't taped until the *Reckoning* sessions, a year later. This is doubly perverse because not only did they record "Burning Down," a song they allegedly disliked, but they did so after recording the song that had evolved from it. It should be noted that the lyrics to both were different on the recorded versions from the original versions. "Ages of You" received only minor alterations, but "Burning Down" was almost completely rewritten. (The lines that I've quoted come from the recorded version.)

Both songs were released separately as B-sides, but in a deliciously ironic twist, they both ended up on the R.E.M. outtakes album, *Dead Letter Office*.

"Windout" is the next in the succession of R.E.M.'s manic rockers, and it's a real screamer. Curiously, despite its lack of subtlety on any level, it really works, driven along primarily by its own energy. There are a few neat little touches, and there is a melody in there somewhere, but for the listener, it's like being bombarded sonically.

"Windout"

One of its chief points of interest is that it is the first of very few songs credited to a co-composer, in this case Jerry Ayers of the Athens band Limbo District. Peter Buck had this to say about him to Craig Rosen, author of *R.E.M.: Inside Out*, "Jerry's an older guy, not like he's ancient, but he's a little older than me. He had been like a Warhol superstar drag guy in the sixties. . . . I think he had this picture of us as this young jail bait boys rock band. So, he wrote 'Windout' and it was kind of like Kim Fowley and The Runaways. He gave us some salacious material that he thought we wouldn't understand, but we did like it."

Knowing that, and bearing in mind the, er, explosive nature of the music, it becomes obvious that the song is a piece of male sexual bragging, or at least it's meant to persuade young, red-blooded men that they're not really tired and that they can do it again! "There's no doubt—if you're feeling fine / No doubt—that you're young and red."

Actually, I rather suspect that the title itself is a double entendre, although it only works on the page. W-i-n-d can be pronounced as either wind, as in gales and the like, or wind, as in winding a clock. In the context of the song, therefore, "windout" can either mean "out of wind," after a bout of sexual congress, or, and I'm ashamed to admit I'm even familiar with this expression, "winding out the python." This is really evolved and sensitive stuff!

This, of course, raises the question: Who actually wrote the lyrics? It's generally assumed that Ayers cowrote them with Stipe, but no one from the band has actually said that. While the sentiments expressed in the song are certainly not beyond Stipe, he was happy to sing it. After all, the words just don't sound like him, and maybe that was liberating. In any case, because of the way R.E.M. publishes all their songs, he would get a credit anyway.

There is, in fact, another set of lyrics. Although they never made it onto *Murmur*, this alternate version was recorded for *Reckoning* but not actually released. As an afterthought, and in what they thought would be a private joke, they cut a second version, albeit with the same backing track. Instead of Michael singing, they used Jefferson Holt, their manager, as lead vocalist and Bertis Downs, their lawyer, as backup. The lyrics on this version are much harder to decipher than the original ones. They are obviously related and follow the same pattern—a shouted "Windout" (or "Findout") followed by a short phrase starting with, "If you're . . ."

However, they are obviously much more salacious than the other lyrics. One line seems to be, "Find out—if you're really bent," and at various points someone shouts, "Go down." Hmm.

Whether these lyrics were improvised by Holt and Downs, I have no idea. Possibly Michael, with or without the others, wrote them especially for this version, or maybe they are Ayers's original lyrics, which the band felt obliged to tone down when they performed it.

The Stipe-sung version of "Windout" appears on the soundtrack to the appalling 1984 movie *Bachelor Party*, but finally found a more appropriate home on *Dead Letter Office*. The other version was never intended for release, although it was bootlegged. It turned up on the 1992 European CD reissue of *Reckoning*, allegedly without the band's consent.

Like "Gardening," "Just a Touch," and "Burning Down," "Windout" can be dated, thanks to various comments by the band, to the early summer of 1980. The next batch of songs is harder to pin down. There are six that appear on a Tyrone's tape recorded January 10, 1981, that do not appear on the October 4, 1980, Tyrone's tape. Consequently, it's a reasonable supposition that all six were composed between the two dates, based on the fact that most of them are demonstrably better than a lot of the material on the earlier tape, and would, therefore, have been performed that night had they been in existence.

"Get on Their Way?" is another song that the band played for a while and dropped, only to revive it much later, newly revised. The new version, with completely rewritten lyrics and retitled "What If We Give It Away?" was released on their 1986 album *Lifes Rich Pageant*. Unfortunately, neither version pleased the band, particularly Peter Buck. He later recalled: "I think it's innocuous, but in a way that would be good if it wasn't on there [i.e., on the album]. . . . You make records and a lot of times what you are doing seems to make sense, but you look back a couple of years and say, 'Why did we do that?'"

Buck is largely right. Aside from one stunning section where they drop into a minor key (also used as an ending flourish on the recorded version) the song is rather plodding. Buck's other comment that a good part of the original had been in $\frac{3}{4}$ time suggests that they had at least tried to brighten the mood on the revised one.

As noted, the lyrics were changed from top to bottom. However, it's hard to make an assessment of the original ones. I am aware of only one tape on which the original song appears (the January '81 Tyrone's show), and the words are all but indecipherable. One line seems to be "People looking for a savior," and there is at least one reference to heaven, possibly: "You can't buy heaven." So it's feasible that "Get on Their Way?" might have religious connotations, but it's really not possible to tell.

Although it's easier to pick out the words of "What If We Give It Away?," it's nearly as impenetrable as its forebear. In part, at least, it seems to be about Stipe's army-brat youth, constantly moving from place to place, or, more likely in this case, staying behind while his father was posted (to Vietnam?), unable to take his family with him: "We're not moving, was it right? / Take the order, sew it on your tie / We couldn't follow, couldn't try."

The title of the revised version may well refer to giving possessions away every time the family moved, but overall, the vagueness of the lyrics subverts any good ideas contained within them. They deserved to have been worked out more fully and to have accompanied a stronger melody.

"Pretty Persuasion" is introduced by a short, jangly arpeggio riff by Buck that for many early fans was the very essence of R.E.M.'s sound. If nothing else, it was instantly recognizable. Fortunately the rest of the song lives up to its opening. It's not quite a screamer like "Windout," but it's certainly no ballad. It is, in fact, a genuinely subtle song, with carefully placed tempo and key changes, a rock-solid backbeat, and a great melody, much of which is handled by the bass.

Apparently, the origins of the song can be traced to a recurring dream of Michael's. In it, he was the photographer for the last ever Rolling Stones' album cover, which reads "Pretty Persuasion." According to Buck, who revealed the dream (rather than Stipe), the Stones themselves were present, "Sitting on a dock with their feet in water."

The dream itself is interesting and could have a variety of meanings. The fact that the photo shoot is for the cover of what is supposed to be the last Stones record, and that Stipe is the photographer, suggests that he is recording their demise.

The water image is curious. Water is traditionally a symbol of the life force, particularly the libido, which certainly evokes the Stones. This has to have been an appealing image to the dreamer: the success and the sexual power. And the fact that it's the Stones' demise, suggests the possibility that, along with a few million others, Stipe would like to be the next Jagger. It's still an ambivalent image, however. In the dream Stipe is the detached observer, the photographer, who could easily reflect the offstage shy, intellectual Stipe. Nonetheless, he undoubtedly finds the dream scene, well, pretty persuasive.

So what else, if anything, did Stipe take from the dream, beyond the title? It almost goes without saying that the lyrics make little or no linear sense, but there are, nonetheless, allusions to all the aspects of the dream.

The opening line, "It's what I want, hurry and buy," would certainly sum up one side of Stipe's dilemma: he wants success and wants people to buy R.E.M. records. Later on he sings "In the light I saw quite a scene there," which seems to refer directly to what he saw in the dream and that he was drawn to it. On the other hand, he "cannot shuffle in this heat, it's all wrong / Try to wear that on my sleeve, it's all wrong." Hearts are what people are prone to wear on their sleeves, which, in this case, would indicate that the private Stipe has reservations about wanting success and revealing himself publicly—something success would certainly bring.

Equally, the heart-on-the-sleeve line might be a more narrow reference to romance, i.e., that Stipe has reservations about revealing his emotions to others. On that basis, the chorus/title might refer to some sort of love triangle: "He's got pretty persuasion / She's got pretty persuasion / Goddamn, pure confusion / He's got pretty persuasion." If that is the case, it's not clear who's persuading whom to do what. It is, indeed, confusing. And there is still the possible connection to the Stones dream, with both the "he" and the "she" in the chorus referring to the sexually ambiguous Jagger.

As with virtually all of Stipe's songs, the lyrics evolved over time. In this case, it seems to have taken him longer than usual to get them to a point where he was satisfied. Consequently, although a live, two-track version of the song was cut during the live two-track session at the end of the main *Murmur* sessions, the song wasn't deemed complete enough to record properly until *Reckoning*. The lyrics quoted above are from the finished version, because the earliest known version features little more than the chorus and some meaningless vocal sounds.

| "Shaking Through" | "Shaking Through" is, in my opinion at least, a rare example of an R.E.M. song that never really worked on stage, however much the band played it. And, relatively speaking, they played it a lot. Most of R.E.M.'s songs work equally well on record or live, even if the two versions are radically different. An exception, *Murmur*'s "Perfect Circle," was not a success live, but they knew it and dropped it after only a handful of performances, at least until they worked out a satisfactory live arrangement some five years later. |

The basic melody of "Shaking Through" is pleasant enough, with some interesting changes and little frills, but it always sounds as though the band were just vamping. Such redeeming qualities as there are come from Stipe's vocal melody line and his impassioned delivery of the song, along with Mills's harmonies. "It's such a long song," Buck once complained, "it seemed like it was eight minutes long." In fact, it was only just over half that length, but you can't argue with someone who had to play it. Mitch Easter, their producer, didn't like it much either, feeling that they could churn out songs like it by the dozen. This is a little unfair, because clearly there was something to "Shaking Through." In fact, it was the simple addition of Mike Mills's piano part on the *Murmur* version that transformed it from a lesser song into an effortlessly majestic one. Unfortunately, it wasn't something they could reproduce on stage.

But what of the lyrics? Once again there are two nearly completely different sets of words: the ones Stipe sang up to the time of the album, and those on the album and after. It's not quite clear if the new ones were written in the studio, but Stipe was certainly singing the old set as late as October 1982, just two months prior to the *Murmur* sessions.

Unfortunately, the lyrics—either set—of "Shaking Through" are among Stipe's most frustrating. The earlier set are almost impossible to decipher on any known rendition, and even the ones on the album are subject to debate among fans. And that's before one even gets close to any kind of interpretation. Quite clearly, though, the song is about something.

In the most general terms it's about childhood and the struggles and fears of growing up. In both versions the chorus is the same: "Shaking through, opportune." The first part certainly implies the fears, but the "opportune" part is highly enigmatic. Maybe "opportune" is just a word that Stipe liked the sound of in that spot. The opening line of the recorded version's first verse also fits in with the childhood theme: "Could it be that one small voice doesn't count in the room?" as does the line about "children of today on parade."

But beyond the lines quoted, one is in very murky territory, in more ways than one. It's been suggested that the song is about, or has implications of, underage sex. The evidence for this are the lines, "Are we grown too far / Taken after rain," and that the title itself suggests a sexual act. Well, perhaps. If so, use of words like "denial," "honor," "yellow," (i.e., cowardly), "geisha," and even "opportune(ity)" do take on extra layers of meaning.

Of possible relevance is one of the few discernible lines in the first version. Instead of "children of today on parade," Stipe sings (by drawing out the relevant syllable) "incest on parade." Of course, incest is not limited to underage sex, nor for that matter is the word always used in a sexual context, but in a song about childhood fears, the implications are probably best not pondered. Except, perhaps, to wonder whether the subject matter of the original version was something Stipe felt the need to tone down or, at least, make even more vague, for the record. One suspects, though, that the incest line apart, it's doubtful that the original version was any more coherent than the later one, so no one would have noticed anyway.

"Sitting Still" When Mitch Easter said that R.E.M. could crank out songs like "Shaking Through" every week, he was right in one sense. They were able, almost effortlessly, to write wonderful and memorable melodies, quite often several within one song. It may have taken the piano part to make the "Shaking Through" melody work, but with "Sitting Still" it was perfect and needed no embellishments. True, it bears some resemblance to the melody of "Gardening at Night," but it remains a fine example of '80s folk-rock.

One surprising aspect of the song is that the lyrics remained consistent from the earliest known performance in January 1981, through the Hib-Tone 45/*Murmur* recording, and at least until 1985. This is odd, given Stipe's usual propensity for changing his lyrics, especially as he later claimed that they were no more than "an embarrassing collection of vowels I strung together some 400 years ago—basically nonsense."

Well, parts of the song are nonsense, at least on a line-by-line basis, but pleasingly so. Lines like "This name I got we all were green / See could stop stop it will red" actually sound fine when sung, and their childlike nature actually fits the overall subject matter of the song. There is the possibility, though, that in the first of those lines Stipe is referring to himself and his family. The word Stipe means, among other things, a short plant stalk, which would, of course, be green.

Stipe's initial inspiration for the song seems to have come from his sister, Cyndy, a teacher of deaf children: "I'm the sun and you can read / I'm the sign and you're not deaf" is not only a fine piece of writing, but it also deftly encapsulates the experience of teaching a deaf child. One of the chief ways we learn to communicate is through hearing, and if you can't hear, you're handicapped. Thus, if deafness is a barrier to communication, teaching someone to sign is to teach them, figuratively, at least, that they aren't deaf.

Marcus Gray, in *It Crawled from the South*, suggests that the child in the song is autistic, citing the line that refers to throwing a fit, as well as the shouted command, "Get away from me," as evidence. He may well

be right, but there also seems to be a religious dimension to the song, of a specifically southern revivalist nature, which might negate Gray's idea.

There are several references in the song to gathering and reaping, which seem distinctly biblical. Gathering also has overtones of the Baptist hymn, "Shall We Gather at the River," especially as, in this case, the word "gather" is followed by "throw a fit," which certainly suggests some sort of ecstatic experience. A religious dimension in any of Stipe's songs is not surprising given that Athens is in the middle of the Bible belt, not to mention that his grandfather was a preacher.

In the end though, the song is primarily about any kind of breakdown in personal communication, especially when people don't listen to each other. On that basis, the "I'm the sun and you can read / I'm the sign and you're not deaf" also has a more adult connotation. The line would then simply mean "You're neither blind nor deaf, look at me and listen to what I'm saying." The line "You can gather when I talk, talk until you're blue," could also be interpreted as part of the same adult conversation. "Gather" in this context means to understand, and "blue" could mean either depressed or [I/we can talk until I/we're] blue in the face. The

Michael Stipe: "An educated young man with an interest in, among other things, literature, film, and art." Mad Hatter Club, Athens, 1983.
(PHOTO BY TERRY ALLEN)

speaker is obviously at the end of his or her tether; in the next line, in a mixture of anger and frustration, he/she shouts, "You could get away from me." The implication being that if the other party doesn't grasp whatever is going on, they should just go. To top it off, the very last line of the song is "I can hear you, can you hear me?"

This interchange sounds remarkably like two lovers arguing, but it could just as easily be a parent or a teacher with a child. This situation might shed a little light on one of the most hotly debated lines in Stipe's entire canon.

The line in question certainly starts with the phrase "Up to par and Katie . . ." but after that we are in the realm of speculation. It might be "Up to bar and Katie buys a kitchen-size, but not Mae Ann." Or perhaps, "Up to par and Katie bars the kitchen signs, but not me in." Or a combination of any of those parts. In 1991, an interviewer for *Select* finally tackled Stipe about the line. His reply was, sadly, only partly illuminating: "It doesn't make any sense. You really don't want to know. . . . I'm trying to think of it. It's a little embarrassing because it's very poorly written 'Up to par and Katie bar.' 'Katie bar the door' is a Southern expression. 'Up to par and Katie bar the kitchen door, but not me in.' That's it."

Unfortunately that's not it. "Katie bar the door," does seem to be a genuine southernism. It implies an authority figure, usually a mother, preventing a misbehaving child from leaving a room prior to administering a thrashing. It's often used more generally to mean "There's going to be trouble." If Stipe had actually written what he told *Select*, it would vaguely tie in with the parent/child encounter, except that in one use of the phrase the child is being told to leave and in the other the door is being barred to prevent his leaving. Whatever Stipe is singing, however, it's not, "Up to par and Katie bars the kitchen door." While I'm still not entirely sure what he is singing, I favor "Up to par and Katie bars the kitchen signs, but not me in." It's the closest to Stipe's supposed line, and I like the repetition of "sign" with the second meaning of "sign language." Whatever it is, it's arresting, but Stipe is right in one respect: It is poorly written.

Equally baffling is the next line. The second half of it, "a waste of time sitting still," is easy to pick out and to interpret. It simply refers to the general hyperactivity of children. The first half of the line is the real puzzler. It might be "Setting trap for lovemaking," or "Sitting child for lovemaking," or, again, some combination of the parts. Then again, Stipe may be saying something quite different and incomprehensible.

Nonetheless, despite Katie and her kitchen door, and a few other weak lines, I think that the lyrics of "Sitting Still" rank with some of Stipe's best. The song works on various levels, but retains a strong overall theme, and some of the individual lines work well, even as poetry. Stipe has also made clever use of puns ("sign" and "gather") and color words (green, red, and blue) that have a broader meaning outside of their literal ones.

Consequently, I find Stipe's feelings toward the song curious. In the same 1991 *Select* interview he says, "I haven't sung that song in five years. I mean sung the real words. I've syllabized it. Is that a real word? When we sing it in concert, I wing it. I don't know the words. I know the sounds. I can approximate them." This, to my mind, is a waste of a perfectly good set of lyrics.

"Radio Free Europe" had everything going for it: It was commercial, yet totally original; pounding, but incredibly melodic with great hooks. In a period when bands sounded crass and manufactured, "Radio Free Europe" sounded as if it were being played by genuine musicians who cared about their work. And, of course, the fact that you couldn't hear most of the lyrics only added to its intriguing qualities.

As a part of the growing R.E.M. songbook, it was an almost-perfect hybrid of their folk-rock delights, like "Gardening at Night," and their aggressive rockers. It's hardly surprising, then, that it became the group's first single. The fact that it wasn't a hit says far more about the taste of the record-buying public than the quality of the music.

But what is it about? In 1985 Stipe told the *NME*, in relation to the Hib-Tone recording of the song, "I purposely did not want any of the lyrics understood. The main reason for that was that I hadn't written any of the words yet. So I just kind of blabbered over the whole single."

In fact, buried though they may be, he is certainly singing real words. In October '83, just after the rerecorded version came out on *Murmur*, Stipe was asked to submit the lyrics to *Song Hits*, which, surprisingly, he did. Not surprising were the legions of bemused fans, unable to make sense of any of it. Stipe then claimed that what he'd given *Song Hits* was a set of joke lyrics. But in fact they are virtually identical to the

"Radio Free Europe"

Hib-Tone single and the *Murmur* versions, as well as being pretty much the same as the earliest known live version, from January '81. Although Stipe has claimed on several occasions that he intended to rewrite it or at least add new verses, it doesn't seem that he has ever done so.

The question is, do the lyrics mean anything, and has it anything to do with the real Radio Free Europe? The answer is: not much. Radio Free Europe was set up after the Second World War by Americans in Berlin, in order to broadcast propaganda to the Eastern Bloc. Apart from the repeated line, "raving station, beside yourself," the only part of the song that might refer to the actual Radio Free Europe is the line about "pushing palaces to fall." Basically, "Radio Free Europe" is just a great title for a song.

However, Peter did have this to say to *Creem*, in 1984:

> Michael and I were talking about weird commercials, and we remembered the spot they used to run for Radio Free Europe where they had that Czech disc jockey talking and then he introduced,
> ". . . de Drivters . . . 'On Broadway.'" When I was a kid I thought that stuff was perfectly natural, but as I got older I thought, isn't that strange—America is spreading cultural imperialism through pop music. . . . So the song related to that, to uncomprehending outsiders listening to rock and roll and not having a clue as to anything about it. I can't imagine someone behind the Iron Curtain figuring out what "On Broadway" means. So it's an evocation of that without mentioning the commercial.

Leaving aside the fact that someone in Russia would find it much easier to work out the meaning of "On Broadway" than "Radio Free Europe" or virtually any R.E.M. song for that matter, do Peter's comments help with understanding the song? Unfortunately not.

If the song suggests anything at all, it's a pledge of solidarity with anybody uprooted and forced to move. The line "Straight off the boat, where to go?" implies refugees to some extent; as does the chorus, if (as I do) you think it is "Calling all in transit," rather than "Calling on," the version that appears in *Song Hits*. Of course, even if it is "Calling all [pas-

sengers] in transit," Michael may have been listening to the announce-
ments in an airport one day and become enamored with the phrase.

Unfortunately, the truth is that the lyrics of "Radio Free Europe" are
largely gibberish. But does knowing that affect the quality of the song?
Certainly not.

The one minor mystery surrounding "Radio Free Europe" is the possibility, albeit an unlikely one, that Stipe originally wrote a completely different set of lyrics for it. In *Talking About the Passion, the Oral History of
R.E.M.*, Gil Ray, sometime drummer with Game Theory, had this to say:
"Either Buck or Stipe told Scott Miller in our band the real words to "Radio
Free Europe" and every now and then we'd do it as a cover because Scott
knew the words." So does "real" equal "different"? Impossible to say.

"White Tornado"

Because "White Tornado" was written purely as an instrumental, it's only
included here for the sake of thoroughness. According to Buck, it was
composed the same day as "Radio Free Europe," and despite playing it
regularly for years, he also noted that they never took it seriously.

As Mitch Easter told Craig Rosen, author of *R.E.M.: Inside Out*, "It
was a throwaway just for fun. . . . Just about every band goes through their
'Let's play [a] surf song' phase. Neither Peter, Buck nor Michael had a hell
of a lot of experience. I think it was just one of those things you discover
on the way to having your band and it did fit in with the campiness of the
time." However, "White Tornado" is nothing for Dick Dale to worry about.

"Romance"

In the liner notes to *Eponymous*, the second R.E.M. compilation album,
Buck claims that "Romance" was "written long ago (with, errr, 'Stumble')
just before first trip to northeast as openers on the Gang of Four tour."
That dates its origins to around the beginning of June '81. Then in an
early '90s interview, Buck claimed it was written the same day as "Radio
Free Europe" and "White Tornado." If the latter is correct, "Romance"
was written no later than the first week of January '81, the date of the first-
known performance of "Radio Free Europe." In the grand scheme of
things, a couple of months either way makes very little difference, but I've
chosen to place it here, between "White Tornado" and "Stumble," so that
it can be viewed as part of either the late 1980 batch of songs or the ones
from the first three months of 1981.

Whenever it was written, it's sadly not classic R.E.M. It's built around a central riff that is either vaguely annoying or pleasantly repetitive, depending on your mood. The whole song has a sort of jogging pace to it that one might even describe as laid-back. "Ages of You" achieves a similar feel much more successfully. Buck described "Get on Their Way?/What If We Give It Away?" as innocuous, but, while I largely agree with him, I think the description is far more apt here. All the more strange, therefore, that for a considerable time it was producer Mitch Easter's favorite R.E.M. song. As Buck later recalled, "On all our albums he would say, 'God, I really wish you guys would do "Romance,"' but we were kind of tired of it."

In fact, they did, allegedly, cut "Romance" with Easter. It's supposed to be a *Murmur* outtake, but it's the one track from those sessions that has never passed into circulation. It's highly unlikely, though, to sound much different from the released version, recorded in 1986, since that one sounds virtually identical to all the known live versions.

If one were to be kind, one would say that Stipe was marking time with the lyrics of "Romance." The central lyrical motif is a kind of chant or mantra, "Easy Come/Easy Go," and the chorus (or it may be the verse—it's hard to tell) ends on each occasion with, "All in all in all in all in all." Stipe is obviously trying to get some sort of mantra-esque repetition going, but it doesn't really come off.

Generally speaking, the words make no sense, but unlike "Radio Free Europe," where they sound as though they must mean something but don't, these just sound like nonsense. However, a later quote, from Buck, about the sources of Stipe's lyrics is obviously relevant: "We decided that we ought to take all these clichés and mutate them. Take fairy tales, old blues phrasings, clichés like 'easy come, easy go,' and just twist them so they were evocative but skewed and more resonant." Well, the theory was good and there's nothing wrong with deliberate nonsense. Edward Lear, the nineteenth-century poet, was a master of nonsense verse. But "Romance," is no "Dong with the Luminous Nose."

If I were to make a stab as to any overall theme in "Romance," it would be sex. And despite the title (which may be ironic), probably casual sex. "Easy come" then means . . . well, enough said. Then there is the inspired couplet, "Mess is yours and call the shot / Even in a parking lot." I rest my case.

Although instantly recognizable as an R.E.M. song, "Stumble" has an unusual structure, even by R.E.M.'s standards: three verses followed by sixteen bars of improvisation, followed by the verse again. Not a chorus in sight. The styles of playing, especially by Buck and Berry, are also quite different from their normal ones. As Buck told author Craig Rosen, "The drums remind me of a Pylon song. Bill had been playing with Love Tractor, so there was the disco-thing in there, too. We were learning how to write songs and it was less traditional than any of our other early stuff. It had these weird kind of broken chords and weird beats."

Mitch Easter was also fond of the song. "I really like it," he later recalled. "To me it had the quintessential R.E.M. vibe at the time. It had the slowed-down ska beat and the thin-sounding, repetitious non-full chord guitar part, and a bass line that moved under it. I thought the way they did that was really clever and cool."

As noted, there was also a section in which they could all improvise, including Stipe. It was always very percussive, and sometimes all the members of the band would simply hit things. Usually it was an excuse for an atonal thrash, with lots of feedback from Buck and with Mills's bass deliberately fracturing the beat. Stipe's contributions ranged from odd noises to random pieces of word play, which were usually inaudible.

For the version of the song that appeared on *Chronic Town*, he recited sections of a late '50s magazine article about jazz life. It's predictably tough to decipher all of it, because it's delivered almost at a whisper, but it fits the tone of the music perfectly. The opening line has been generally decoded as: "It was round about midnight—hipster town," which is good, but I think he's saying "hipster time," which is even better.

Stipe's own lyrics, as opposed to the magazine quotes, are masterpieces of brevity; if nothing else they are a long way from the extended rambling of "Radio Free Europe." There is no chorus, but the verse is divided into three distinct sections. The first contains the line "We'll stumble through the yard," which is repeated four times, except that at the end of the third time, Stipe changes "yard" to the spelled-out "A-P-T." A-P-T has been generally accepted as a reference to the Athens Party Tape (or Telegraph), a telephone message service set up by Michael Lachowski of the Athens band Pylon to keep the locals abreast of upcoming raves. Of course, A-P-T could just as easily be the standard abbreviation for apartment—which, although more prosaic, makes more sense. On a literal

level one can imagine the members of R.E.M. stumbling around, probably partying, which might account for the Athens Party Tape reference. On a slightly more poetic level, I think that Stipe is referring to stumbling through life, which at this stage he probably thought he was (and may still do, for that matter).

The next section is tougher to decipher. He's probably saying, "Force fields, explorer racing home, the ancient star / Yellow mixed with golden hues / Scan the graveyard dead there be." Evocative images to be sure, but do they mean anything in the context of the song? The only thing I can grasp from it is the idea of stumbling through life toward death, which at least explains the graveyard. And the only link I can come up with between "force fields," "explorers," and "stars," is *Star Trek* or something similar. But what it means and what it has to do with the first part of the song, or the "golden hues," I've no idea.

The last section is simply the phrase "Ball and chain" repeated four times. The phrase might refer to the stereotypical manacled ghost, who may very well be wandering around a graveyard, but it might also refer metaphorically to being shackled. You would certainly stumble through life if enchained.

Despite their overall lack of clarity, I like the words, and they complement the music splendidly. Stipe obviously liked them as well. Almost two years after writing them, he told a radio interviewer in New Orleans that, to date, they were still his favorite lyrics. My only real regret is that he didn't write more. The one verse is repeated three times before the improvised section and once afterward. One suspects that, for Stipe, it was a deliberate choice, a demonstration of the validity of repetition. But change is good, too.

"Carnival of Sorts (Box Cars)"

Like "Stumble," "Carnival of Sorts" demonstrates a darker side of R.E.M.'s music. However, unlike "Stumble," which maintains a somber, almost ethereal tone more or less throughout, "Carnival of Sorts" demonstrates a far greater range of emotions. The music runs the gamut from slow, almost gentle folk-rock to blinding crescendos, with Stipe's voice appropriately moving from a whisper to a howl. All the way through, however, there is a distinct undertone of menace, which is conveyed not only by the voices but also by the music that underpins them.

Michael and Peter, shortly after the band signed with IRS in 1982.
(PHOTO BY TERRY ALLEN)

For once there is little argument over the actual lyrics, just the customary ones as to their meaning. In this case, they are more than usually impressionistic. But taking the main part of the title as starting point, it's fairly obvious that we are dealing with a carnival visiting a small, rural town.

The idea that there is something distinctly menacing about a carnival, something evil lurking below its raffish surface, is by no means new. In the late '40s, science-fiction and fantasy writer Ray Bradbury published a collection of short stories entitled *Dark Carnival* and later a novel on the subject entitled *Something Wicked This Way Comes*. The latter work features, apart from the usual catalog of freaks, a carousel that when speeded up or reversed, will, accordingly, increase or lower the age of the rider. The carousel is run by the appropriately named Mr. Dark, in whose hands this potential elixir of life becomes an instrument of temptation and evil. The other work that comes to mind is the 1962 film *Carnival of Souls*, a fascinating and surreal horror story, part of which is set in an abandoned carnival. If nothing else, one assumes that it provided Stipe with his title.

Of course, I'm speculating, because the lyrics are decidedly minimalist. Nonetheless, some of the images are powerful. The action takes place in a "chronic town," which certainly suggests a place rife with corruption. In fact, the word "chronic" derives from the Greek and simply means "time," or "over time," but the modern use of the word (e.g., in the phrase "chronic illness" or "chronic bad habits") combined with the original, indicates that this town has been in some sense "sick" over a long period and will continue to be so.

"Poster torn" could refer to one of two things: either the town has been badly neglected, and old, yellowing posters are left to flutter in the, no doubt, dusty wind. Alternatively, the good citizens of the town may have torn down a portion of the carnival poster to show their disgust at the altogether un-Christian entertainments on offer. It's possible that this last image could tie in with the line "Gentlemen don't get caught." It's not clear, though, in which sense this phrase is being used. It could be used as a plea, "Gentlemen, please don't get caught," or as a flat statement, "Gentlemen never get caught"—implying that other, working-class men might get caught. But caught at what?

Well, possibly the infamous hoochie-coochie shows that took place after the carnival had theoretically closed for the night. These were basically strip shows, but could, by all accounts, get a good deal raunchier. In the rural parts of the Bible belt, such a show would undoubtedly offend sections of the populous, even in a "Chronic town," and cause them to tear down posters and maybe a good deal more. This might also explain the "secret stigma" mentioned in the first line. Any man known to have attended a hoochie-coochie show would certainly be stigmatized, secretly or otherwise.

For years I thought that in the "boxcars" section of the song, Mike Mills's harmony part was "are burning," making the whole line, "Boxcars are burning out of town." This gave rise to a wonderful image of an uprising of the townspeople, angry and wielding torches, as at the end of a *Frankenstein* movie. One can envision them setting fire to the carnival equipment, which had been loaded into boxcars in the rail yard on the outskirts of town. However, after repeated listening, I have recently become convinced that they are singing "boxcars are pulling out of town," which rather puts the damper on my scenario. Although I suppose the carnival could be leaving hurriedly to avoid being burned. It's just a thought.

More interesting, perhaps, than all this speculation is the probability that Stipe wrote the lyrics so that they were easy to play with afterward. Much of the song is composed of two- or three-word phrases, which Stipe can move about almost at will. There is a tendency to think of the recorded lyrics as being the definitive ones, but in Stipe's case this is certainly not true. Usually though, the lyrics are consistent within one version. In the case of "Carnival of Sorts" he breaks them down and reassembles the lyrics within the one song. Thus, even on the *Chronic Town* version, the last verse contains all of the elements of the first verse, but completely rearranged. And in live versions he changed them around even more.

Bill Berry initially hated "Carnival of Sorts" and claimed he would never play it. His refusal didn't last long, which was a good thing for us, because "Carnival of Sorts" is one of R.E.M.'s strongest songs.

Musically, "Wolves, Lower" is as superficially bright and cheerful as anything R.E.M. wrote during this period. It's upbeat, full of bright ringing arpeggios on the guitar, and has a nice fat bass line. The only jarring note comes from the instrumental section, which, although more concise than the one on "Stumble," still leaves them room to turn the beat around and

"Wolves, Lower"

come up with wacky atonal noises. On virtually every known performance of the song, this section is the same length, and no matter what kind of musical strangeness they'd been into, they all jump back into the riff, as one, with effortless grace.

But while the music may sound cheerful, the lyrics tell a different story. They are decidedly dark and arguably primal. Most writers on R.E.M. have made the leap from the wolves and house mentioned in the song to the children's stories of "The Three Little Pigs" and "Little Red Ridinghood," citing, as evidence, Stipe's known fascination with childhood in general and fairy tales in particular. (Technically, neither "The Three Little Pigs" or "Little Red Ridinghood" are fairy tales; they are beast fables.)

Stipe is undoubtedly alluding to one or both of these in "Wolves, Lower," but to equate the song with the modern censored versions of these fables is to miss the point. While "The Three Little Pigs" probably hasn't changed that much over the years, "Little Red Ridinghood" has. In common with most of the other old beast fables, it was heavily bowdlerized in the nineteenth century. Before then it was extremely bloodthirsty. Ridinghood herself was rather graphically eaten by the wolf, and some authorities believe that in the earliest German versions there are suggestions that the wolf rapes Ridinghood before eating her. In fact, the whole story (including Little Red Ridinghood's name) is something Freudians have a field day with.

It's this sexual aspect of Ridinghood's wolf that begins to explain Stipe's wolves, or at least the narrator-as-character's. The song's central metaphor seems to be that of the wolf as the sexual predator in men. However, unlike the wolf in the tale, who is, to say the least, unleashed, the narrator seems to be attempting to control his "wolf." An inner dialog seems to be taking place. "Suspicion yourself," the narrator is saying to himself, that is, "be on guard against your basic impulses. There are things in a civilized society that you just don't do." The next phrase, "don't get caught," would seem to indicate the opposing voice saying, "Yes, do it, but don't get caught" (an echo, perhaps, of the "Gentlemen don't get caught" line in "Carnival of Sorts").

The "Suspicion yourself" line is then repeated, followed by "let us out." And if that isn't sufficiently self-explanatory, the next line seems to spell it out: "In a corner garden, wilder, lower wolves" sounds remarkably like a description of potentially out-of-control male genitalia. Which brings to mind a comment made by Tommy, the alien who ends up in a teenage boy's body, in the TV comedy *3rd Rock from the Sun*. In relation to the sudden urges brought on by puberty, he complains, "I've got a circus in my shorts." Tommy is obviously younger than the narrator of "Wolves, Lower," but the situation is similar: the narrator's problem is just bigger.

The next line, "Here's a house to put wolves out the door," is more ambiguous. It would seem to indicate that the narrator has located an outlet (the house) for his urges. However, the next new line, with the repeated phrase "House in order," suggests that the house is the narrator, or at least the part of him that's relevant, and that he's got it under control. The only way to make sense of both lines is if the "houses" mentioned are not one and the same. Accepting that makes it easier to see that the narrator's interior debate is ongoing.

The last line, "Down there they're rounding a posse to ride," is also ambiguous. It might suggest that the narrator's urges have been, or will be, reined in. Alternatively, it could mean exactly the opposite. Almost any metaphor with "ride" in it indicates sexual activity of some description. The ambiguity is no doubt deliberate because this particular inner debate has no resolution.

It should be noted that there is at least one other, completely different, interpretation of the lyrics of "Wolves, Lower." In this one the wolves are the predatory record companies from whom the band have to protect themselves. In order to do this they have to be "suspicious" and to "get their house in order." Even though it only explains part of the song, it does have a certain prosaic logic to it. I could be wrong, but I don't think Michael would write such a complex and image-rich song on such a mundane, if troublesome, subject.

Either way, I think it's one of Stipe's more extraordinary lyrics. And unlike "Stumble," which would have benefited from an extra verse or two, "Wolves, Lower" is fine just the way it is. Of somewhat lesser importance is the fact that the full title is a joke. It's really just "Wolves," but Stipe apparently fancied having a title with an unnecessary comma in it, like the Stones' "Paint It, Black."

Even in its most naked form, live, "Laughing" is one of the most achingly beautiful songs in the R.E.M. catalog. The layered acoustic guitars of the

"Laughing"

Peter Buck ponders the lyrics of "Gardening at Night." London, November 1983.

(PHOTO BY EVA HUNTE)

Murmur version simply emphasize the soft ringing quality of the onstage renditions. Despite the "folky" nature of the song, however, the structure is a departure from their earlier folk-rock pieces, like "Gardening at Night" and "Sitting Still." The melodies of those songs owed something, whether acknowledged or not, to the Byrds. With "Laughing," R.E.M. was breaking new ground. The beat frequently gets turned around; at other times the band stops on a dime and changes the melody line, and the whole song has a slightly skewed and unsettling feel.

Unconsciously, perhaps, they devised a way of marrying the melodic, but invariably linear, qualities of the best '60s music with the angular qualities of the more innovative punk bands, for whom melody was not the primary motivation. The result, when added to the unique qualities of R.E.M., was what came to define their sound, at least for the next two or three years.

The subject matter of "Laughing" has prompted more controversy than probably any other R.E.M. song: not the lyrics themselves—which are, for once, not in dispute—but their meaning. Presumably in recognition of this controversy, Stipe has talked a lot about "Laughing" over the years. What he has invariably discussed, however, is what inspired him to write the song, which proves to be at least four different things. Only rarely has he touched on its meaning. Still, you use what you can get.

When I interviewed Stipe in 1983 he told me:

> The first line is about Laocoön, a Greek mythological figure who had two sons; all three were devoured by serpents. It was a popular theme in Renaissance painting. It's also like the photos you see of the women in Nazi Germany. You know, the woman with the shaved head, clutching her baby, running from all these people who are laughing at her. But that's a real expansive definition of the song. There's also John Barth's novel *End of the Road*, where a statue of Laocoön features heavily. Oh! I did change the gender in the song, from a man to a woman.

The first thing to say is that, if Stipe had never told us that the character in the song is Laocoön, we would never have known. The name is usually pronounced to rhyme, more or less, with "cow-moon"; what Stipe sings is closer to "Le-wok-a-won." Laocoön appears in Virgil's *Aeneid*, in the section dealing with the last days of the Trojan war and he is chiefly remembered for his role in the wooden horse debacle, which brought about the end of the war. Originally, Laocoön had been the priest of Apollo but became, instead, the acting priest of Neptune, after the previous incumbent had been stoned to death for alleged neglect of duty. When the Greeks arrived with the wooden horse, claiming that they'd had enough of the war and that the horse was a parting gift, Laocoön was the only Trojan who didn't trust them. He then uttered the famous phrase, which, roughly translated, means "Beware Greeks bearing gifts."

Shortly afterward, Laocoön, along with his two sons, was on the shore preparing a sacrifice when two giant sea serpents, sent by Neptune, appeared and either crushed or devoured all three of them. It is this scene that is usually represented in paintings and sculptures. The most famous depiction is a Greek sculpture from the Hellenic period, rather than Renaissance, and is owned by the Vatican. It's this one that Stipe probably had in mind.

Anyway, the Trojans were immediately convinced that Laocoön's death was punishment for blasphemously rejecting the horse. They dragged it into the city, and the rest is history, or at least myth.

The key line in the song about Laocoön's fate is "Martyred, misconstrued." He was certainly misconstrued by the Trojans. They failed to understand both his rejection of the horse and the reason for his death. To call him a martyr is stretching the definition a little. Technically, a martyr willingly accepts punishment, usually death (although not always), rather than recant a stated position or an article of faith. More generally, it can refer to anybody who out of guilt, low self-esteem, or sheer perversity allows themselves to be punished or ridiculed. We generally admire the "genuine" martyr, even if we disagree with their articles of faith. We are, at best, suspicious of the other sort.

If the Trojans, or the snakes, had told Laocoön to recant his stand over the horse and he'd refused, resulting in his death, that would have been an act of martyrdom. As it happened he simply was killed by agents of a god who, at that particular moment, was backing the other side in a war.

Stipe's second inspiration, the shaven-headed woman clutching a baby, actually fits more of the song. However, it should be pointed out that Stipe probably wasn't remembering the scene correctly. What he seems to have had in mind were persecuted Jewish women in Germany. However, the famous photos are of women who had given somewhat more than usual "aid and comfort" to the enemy during the occupation of France. On that basis they may have been martyrs, but they command less sympathy from us than if they were persecuted Jews. These women subsequently had to run the gauntlet of the townspeople, who hurled abuse, verbal and physical, and laughed derisively at them.

Curiously, the phrase Stipe uses is "Run the gamut," usually meaning to go through a whole range of emotions, for instance, rather than the more literal "run the gauntlet." One assumes his word choice was deliberate and not a simple mistake. If deliberate, he is presumably implying, as well, that the women had gone through a catalog of emotional states, which they undoubtedly had.

What the women are seeking is sanctuary, which, to my mind, is the other major theme of the song. There are lines suggesting this throughout: "In a room, lock the door, latch the room"; "settled new";

and "find a place fit to laugh." Sanctuary, in the sense of a place of safe-ty, derives from the medieval right of being protected from prosecution and/or persecution for as long as one was inside a church. In a more general way, it is also a place where you can laugh, if only as an emotional release.

The connections between "Laughing" and Stipe's third inspiration, Barth's satirical novel *End of the Road*, are a little more tenuous. The book, written in the late '50s, concerns a young man, Jake Horner, who has had some sort of nervous breakdown prior to finishing his doctorate in English Lit. He finds sanctuary of varying degrees in a series of places. The first is a decidedly progressive mental hospital, located in the countryside. His doctor convinces him that he should find a job teaching prescriptive grammar. He lands a position, but before taking it he rents a room in a house: his second sanctuary. Jake has very definite ideas of what he requires in a room: it should be high-ceilinged and high-windowed, in other words "lanky," the rather odd word that Stipe uses to describe the room in "Laughing."

One of Horner's few possessions is a small reproduction of the Laocoön statue, but, beyond the coincidence, it doesn't seem to connect with the song. Its primary function in the book is as a mildly comic device. Horner looks at it from time to time, hoping for some enlightenment, but all it ever does is grimace at him.

The school, a small private establishment, provides another sanctuary for Horner. Early on he is befriended by another teacher, Joe Morgan, and his wife, Rennie. It is their triangular, somewhat dysfunctional, relationship that forms the core of the novel. Horner has an affair with the wife (another form of sanctuary, perhaps) but it's a highly unsatisfying liaison for both parties. In fact, Rennie claims to hate Jake and his motivation for the affair is vague.

Despite the fact that Rennie's husband physically abuses her, or perhaps because of it, she is unable to lie to him and tells him about the affair. In an act of perversity, he insists that she continue the relationship. She won't go against his will, but since she hates Jake, she is in a bind. She refuses Jake's offer that they only pretend they are still having sex, because that would involve lying to her husband. Almost inevitably, she becomes pregnant and Jake arranges an abortion, which was still an illegal procedure when the book was written. Rennie dies during the operation, which necessitates a cover-up. The husband claims that she was depressed and had the abortion without his knowledge. Jake isn't mentioned. Ironically, although the school hushes up the incident, they decide to fire the husband anyway. Jake is off the hook but, wracked with guilt, quits his job and leaves town.

By the end of the book, it's quite easy to view all three of the main characters as martyrs, although they only become so through highly suspect and perverse motives. And, despite the fact that all three indulge in lengthy discussions about the nature of their various relationships within the triangle, everybody misconstrues everybody else. On the whole, from the reader's point of view, they are a pretty unsympathetic group.

The last source of inspiration for the song, Nathaniel Hawthorne's novel *The Scarlet Letter*, was not mentioned by Stipe until much later. In fact, what he said was that "Laughing" was a "rewrite" of *The Scarlet Letter*, rather than an inspiration, which, coupled with the lapse of time before he made this announcement, suggests that he read the novel sometime after writing the song, and only then was struck by the similarity of the themes.

Whatever the truth of the matter, there is no doubt that the parallels between the novel and the song are striking. The novel was published in 1850 and set in the Puritan New England of an earlier time. Before the novel opens, the main character, Hester Prynne, a married woman whose husband has gone missing, has had a brief affair with the local minister, Reverend Dimmesdale, and borne a child. This is a major crime against the Puritan code and one for which she might have been put to death. At the start of the novel, however, she is released from prison with her baby, but immediately has to run the gauntlet of the townspeople. She is more or less banished, but is able to find sanctuary ("settled new" is the relevant line in the song) in a small cottage beyond the town, at the edge of the forest.

She is forced to wear a huge scarlet "A" (for adulteress), which she herself embroiders on her dress, as a mark of her sin. The scarlet letter becomes nothing less than a badge of defiance. Ironically, because it is so perfectly made, it also becomes a source of admiration within the otherwise hostile community, and Hester is able to make a living as a seamstress.

Hester is most certainly a martyr, if for no other reason than that she refuses to name the baby's father. In another ironic twist, Dimmesdale, whose feelings of guilt have overwhelmed him, publicly announces his sin, just before he is to leave America with Hester and their, by then, seven-year-old daughter. He promptly dies. The novel ends when it is revealed that Hester's husband, who has known all along about Hester's plight, has been posing as a doctor and slowly poisoning Dimmesdale. Nonetheless, he forgives her, or at least her daughter, to whom he leaves a fortune. All in all, a lot of martyrdom, perhaps, but in the character of Hester Prynne, at least, we find one of the great heroines.

Whether any of the themes of the song—martyrdom, being misconstrued, seeking sanctuary—apply in any measure to the song's author is a matter of speculation. The fact that Stipe managed to find all of those themes in so many different sources suggests, at the very least, that they struck a very loud chord with him. One thing that may or may not be relevant is the fact that in early, pre-*Murmur*, live versions of the song, Stipe always sang "In my room." On the album, and later on when they performed the song onstage, it became simply "In a room."

"9-9"

"9-9" has been described as "explosive" and "discordant," which does, pretty much, sum it up. All three musicians seem to wind themselves up in order to burst out with staccato blasts from their respective instruments, not necessarily at the same time. Comparisons have been made between this song and the music of bands like Gang of Four. As Mitch Easter told author Craig Rosen: "Right away they were seen as being really melodic, which at the time was a bit negative with some people. ["9-9"] was probably written as the song that was going to be the opposite of that."

That may be true, but they'd already written "Just a Touch," and "Windout," neither of which were exactly cozy folk ballads. There is a more avant-garde, dissonant quality to "9-9," however, which sets it apart structurally from those two. Conversely, there is a melody somewhere in there, primarily supplied by Stipe's vocal line, which probably indicates that R.E.M. was incapable of writing a song without distinctive hooks, however hard they tried.

Lyrically, "9-9" is one of the three songs from this era that Stipe has described as "complete babbling" (the other two being "Radio Free

Europe" and "Sitting Still"). With "9-9," Stipe went even further and suggested that it was deliberately written and sung so that the only words you can hear are "conversation fear," adding, somewhat glibly, "that's what the song's about."

In fact, other than the spoken introduction, the lyrics are no more indecipherable than any of the others from this time, even if they are pretty obtuse. If there is a clue to part, at least, of what the song is about, it's in that spoken introduction. Although Stipe seems to have varied it from time to time, one constant seems to be the first line: "Steady repetition is a compulsion mutually reinforced." I have a strong suspicion that this a quotation, but if it is, I have been unable to discover the source.

It brings to mind two things. The first is Stipe's fascination with language and the probability that he was aware of semiotics, that somewhat pretentious branch of linguistics. A full discussion of semiotics is out of place here, and anyway I've never been sure that I fully understand it. However, one of its tenets holds that repetition itself is significant and can point out something that the writer wants you, the reader/listener, to notice. This is a technique that Stipe certainly employs frequently in all his work.

Oddly enough, there is little repetition in "9-9" except, of course, in the title itself. It might also be worth noting that when spoken, the title is German for "no-no," and that the ninth letter of the alphabet is "I," making it "I-I" and, therefore, possibly "Me-Me."

The other thing that the first line brings to mind is Freud's theory of repetition compulsion, which, briefly stated, is the blind impulse to reenact earlier emotional experiences, irrespective of any disadvantage that doing so might bring. Theoretically, once the early emotional experience is consciously acknowledged, the impulse to repeat it dies away.

Although it's only in the vaguest and most impressionistic terms, what Stipe may be describing in the song is a relationship based on repetition compulsion. There are references to "lies," "twisting tongues" (which suggests an inability to communicate verbally), and "conversation fear." Fear, or more exactly the fear of dealing with the situation (hence necessitating the repetition compulsion), may also be indicated by the lines "gotta stripe down his back / All nine yards down her back"— assuming, that is, that the stripes (or streaks) are yellow, a yellow streak down the back being the figurative designation of a coward.

Bertis Downs, lawyer and sometime backup vocalist. (PHOTO BY SANDRA LEE-PHIPPS)

The inability, or the lack of desire, to deal with this communication breakdown is also present in the lines, "Give me a couple / Don't give me a couple of pointers." In this context those lines might mean, "Give me a clue as to what's going on, but on reflection, don't bother." Don't bother because everything becomes "lies and conversation fear."

As so often with Stipe's lyrics, these are only impressions suggested by the images in the song. The words are far too vague for one to be definitive. However, for Stipe to regard "9-9" as "complete babbling" is overly dismissive. There is undoubtedly something going on.

"Skank"

"Skank" first appears on a tape from May 1981, but the band had been toying with the ideas it embraces for some time. In some respects "Skank" was never more than a loose jam, but its fractured rhythms, weird chords, and improvised lyrics were clearly derived from earlier experiments. Partly, it came from the band's extrapolated reading of "Gloria"—not so much the original '60s version by Them, but the more fragmented version by Patti Smith, which always included her own improvised poetry. R.E.M.'s extended version would frequently segue into other songs, the lyrics of which Stipe would invariably improvise.

The more direct ancestor to "Skank" was the improvised midsection of "Stumble," taken to its logical conclusion. Although the band continued to perform "Stumble," after they'd come up with "Skank," they would sometimes abandon the improvised section of "Stumble" (and the last run-through of the verse) and go straight into "Skank."

Despite the variations of "Skank" from performance to performance, it usually started quietly with Buck playing reggae style half-chords. Over the music Stipe would intone in an even voice the "lyrics." These, too, varied from show to show, but he would commonly start the proceedings with the line, "There's a marble table made of glass, at the end of the table there's a photograph." From there they would build to a series of crescendos that involved lots of feedback from Buck and Mills plus howling by Stipe.

Even on gigs where he used the marble-table motif, Stipe would go on to improvise wildly, often describing whatever was going on around him. Occasionally he would improvise from start to finish, sometimes at length, sometimes minimally, such as the night that the lyrics consisted solely of the repeated phrase "The opposite of plethora is dearth."

Although R.E.M. did demo "Skank" on one occasion—during the pre-*Reckoning* sessions in November 1983—it seems that they never considered cutting a "proper" version with a view to releasing it. This is a shame because, despite its all-around wackiness, "Skank," on a good night, was one of their most exciting numbers. Maybe they felt that it only worked in a live setting, its inherent spontaneity getting lost in the studio.

The writing of "Skank" represented the end of one of R.E.M.'s most productive periods. With the increased pressures of touring, their composition rate dropped dramatically, and, as far as is known, the next performance of a new song, "1,000,000," was not until October 1981.

"1,000,000"

Chronologically, "1,000,000" (pronounced "a million") was the last written and, in some ways, the least innovative of the songs used on the *Chronic Town* EP. Not that there's anything wrong with it. It's a perfectly fine hard rocker, with another excellent hook. But it has neither the majesty, the quirkiness, nor the sheer power of their best compositions of the previous year.

It's worth noting that "1,000,000" must have come together quickly, especially the lyrics, because the earliest known version is the one used on the EP. Although the band usually settled on the musical parts early on, Stipe would frequently rewrite chunks of a song over time, until he was happy with it. These writing habits would explain why a song like "Pretty Persuasion," despite being written as early as December 1980, was not recorded until early 1984. These large changes to a song are different from the improvised changes Stipe would make onstage as the mood took him. In the case of "1,000,000," it's possible, of course, that Stipe believed that the lyrics were as good as they were ever going to get (not that they were so wonderful that they could not be improved upon).

The basic conceit of the song is that the narrator is living in a grave, metaphorical or literal, and is, therefore, in some sense, dead. Death in this instance is a metaphor, presumably for isolation: "Secluded in a marker stone." The narrator's attitude to his isolation is somewhat ambiguous. Assuming he wants to be left alone, it further suggests the notion of "the outsider," the person who feels himself different from the rest of the society and enjoys living on its margins, "all along the ruin." It would be fascinating to know whether Stipe had read Albert Camus's *L'Etranger*, the classic study of the outsider, shortly before writing "1,000,000."

Equally, the narrator may hate his isolation. The "I could live a million years" line might not be youthful boasting but a cry of desperation. As is all too common with Stipe's lyrics, there is no way of knowing. However, unlike "Wolves, Lower," where the song's unresolved argument is one of the things that makes it so good, with "1,000,000," the ambiguity is more than a little frustrating, even if some of the grave imagery is powerful.

There is a school of thought which believes that Michael is singing "all along the chain" rather than "all along the ruin." This reading coupled with Stipe's frequent and emphatic "I don't drink the water!" at the end of many live versions have convinced a number of R.E.M. scholars that "1,000,000" is, in part, a comment on the food chain and pollution.

"Jazz Lips"

Technically, "Jazz Lips" is the next known R.E.M. composition and dates from October 1981. However, because it was essentially a studio creation, including the lyrics, it will be discussed in Chapter 3.

"Catapult"

With its punchy bass, pounding drum beat, and fluttery guitar, "Catapult" is one of the most uplifting and catchy songs in the R.E.M. catalog. It also exhibits a subtle country influence. As Buck recalled in 1984: "A lot of country guitar playing is really neat. It's melodic and pithy and not chord oriented, without being jerk-off guitar solos. I stick things in all the time that are real country. That's a country lick right before the chorus in 'Catapult.'"

Almost unique among Stipe's efforts of this period, the lyrics are discernable, the overall theme is readily apparent, and it almost makes sense on a line-by-line basis. Clearly, it's a song about childhood. However, unlike "Sitting Still" where the child voice of the song is set in the present, the scenes portrayed in "Catapult" are surely drawn from Stipe's memory and are quite definitely set in the past. He lets us know this in the first line, "We were little boys / We were little girls."

The song is full of the things that concern young kids: pleading with parents not to turn off the TV at nine o'clock; the desperate feeling that you might be missing out on something; and all-encompassing fear, rational or otherwise, that could strike at any time. In the case of the song, the fear is generated by the howl of the catapult rope and its possible consequences, with the narrator, "cowered [or possibly 'coward'] in a hole, opie mouth." "Opie" may simply be a child's variant of "open." He may also be referring to Opie, the character played by the young Ron Howard on the *Andy Griffith Show*, which Stipe might have seen in reruns. Less likely, but even more intriguing, is the possibility that "opie" is an oblique reference to the British writers Iona and Peter Opie, who, for the last thirty years or so, have been acknowledged experts on the lore, language, and games of children, as well as on the history of fairy tales.

For once, "Catapult" seems to be a straightforward song, a recollection of childhood in general, with a specific memory of the catapult itself. The only deeper interpretation is the possibility that the narrator/Stipe is looking back and wondering if he missed something that would help him deal with the complexities of adult life. Michael was certainly fascinated with how the incidents of childhood can make themselves felt in adulthood. As Buck told *Zigzag* in 1984, "maybe [it's] because he had a weird childhood himself, a kind of time and innocence lost." Responding to a question on the same subject during another interview, Buck added, "Michael had a very strong family life. He has two sisters and sees his family a lot. The family in that time [his childhood] was real important to him, and that comes through in the lyrics...."

It may be worth noting that around the time *Murmur* was released, Stipe told a radio interviewer that the song "has a definite meaning for me and a totally different one for the others."

Curiously enough, although R.E.M. played "Catapult" live for several years, it was never a band favorite. Maybe parts of it, especially the "We were little boys / We were little girls" lines, were just too insipid for them. Equally, their growing distaste for the song may have resulted from their experience of recording it with producer Stephen Hague, in December 1982, an event detailed in Chapter 4.

In 1987, in a revealing section of a *Musician* article, the members of R.E.M. were asked which of their songs they would categorically refuse to play. Stipe's reply was, "'Catapult.' Actually, I would do it as a joke."

Incidentally, "Catapult" was written in time to be tried out when the band went into the studio in January 1982.

"West of the Fields," along with "Pilgrimage," was probably written around March or April 1982; certainly both were ready in time to be performed by late April. "West of the Fields," for better or worse, combines just about every element that R.E.M. had put into a song up until then—not that it actually ended up sounding like any of them.

Although he was thinking in part about the recorded version, Buck's later comments on the writing of the song explain this patchwork approach: "In those days, if [one of our songs] didn't have three different bridges, and a separate A and B section before the chorus, it just wasn't any good. Maybe it's because I wasn't a great player, but I felt I had to put in all those extra chords. 'West of the Fields' is a perfect example—there must be fifteen chords in that song. So we wanted no lead guitar and no heavy punk—just a fast weird folk-rock record with tons of overdubs."

Obviously, Buck, of all people, is entitled to his opinion, but I, for one, find the elaborate structures and multiple chord changes a good part of what I like about early R.E.M. songs. Perhaps they were able to get away with it precisely because they were still journeyman songwriters, anxious to experiment, but redeemed from pretentiousness by a degree of naiveté. Maybe there is too much going on in "West of the Fields," but I still think it's an excellent song. I agree with Mitch Easter, who described it as "kind of a cool, dramatic song."

The song lyrics grew out of a trip Michael made to New Orleans. It would be good to know what specifically sparked the words because there is repeated reference in the song to "Elysian." The few writers who have commented on it have, quite rightly, mentioned the Elysian Fields of Greek mythology. But it seems likely that Stipe's initial inspiration was New Orleans itself, where there is an Elysian Fields Avenue, as well as several businesses bearing the name, including the Elysian Fields Animal Hospital and an Elysian Fields Gas Station.

The various New Orleans Elysian Fields, however, have little relevance to the song as it stands, whereas the mythological ones do. The mythological Elysian Fields were the eternal resting place for a select few heroes favored by the gods. Essentially, it was paradise. According to Virgil the Fields were located in the underworld, beyond the palace of Hades,

"'Wobbling through?' No. 'Teetering through?' that doesn't work. 'Shaking through?' Yeah, that'll do." The artist finds inspiration. (Photo by Laura Levine)

on the west bank of the River Lethe. Homer merely said that it was located at the world's end.

Although the mythical Elysian Fields are clearly being referred to in the song, the connection is vague. The song would appear to be about death and/or dreaming, two states that are traditionally related to each other. In some cultures death is even regarded as nothing more than an extended dream. The lines, "Dreams of Elysian, to assume are gone when we die," and "Listen through your eyes when we die," at least suggest that we are dealing with both topics in some way. And the repeated phrase "Long Gone" certainly speaks of death if one accepts the idea that going "West of the Fields" is to die. In this context the title probably refers to Virgil's locating the Fields on the west side of the Lethe, although the Fields themselves were paradise, not whatever was west of them. If Stipe had called the song "West of the Lethe," it might have made things a bit clearer.

The one line that seems to be totally out of context is "The animals, how strange. Try, try to stick it in." The image suggested by the line is either violent or sexual or both. But who is doing what and to whom (or what) I have no idea and would perhaps rather not know.

Ultimately, the song has to go in the wonderful-imagery, might-mean-something-profound-but-really-difficult-to-tell group of Stipe lyrics. In fact, Stipe didn't write all of "West of the Fields." He was assisted by his friend Neil Bogan, who thus became the second outsider to receive a writing credit on an R.E.M. song.

"Pilgrimage"

On a superficial level, at least, "Pilgrimage" bears a relationship to "Laughing," if only in the sense that they are both in R.E.M.'s recently discovered "skewed folk-rock" style. They also start instrumentally with odd little bass and drum figures. In the case of "Pilgrimage," Buck joins in after a few bars, but he plays the same riff as Mills and in a very low register. Berry meanwhile is playing in double time.

It's often useful, but most especially here, to know which came first, the lyrics or the music, because with "Pilgrimage" the music exactly matches words. In the first section, which includes the line "Your hate, clipped and distant," the rhythm is decidedly clipped. It only smoothes out, and at the same time speeds up, at the line that precedes the chorus, "Your pilgrimage has gained momentum." Because it's highly unlikely to be a coincidence, this reverse onomatopoeia must be regarded as a fascinating device, and as far as I know the only time they employed it. It's also only when they speed up that you can pick out Buck's part, when he starts vamping chords. Prior to that it sounds remarkably as though he's playing another bass guitar.

A pilgrimage is usually understood to mean the journey of a religious person to a holy place, and there is, certainly, a religious component to this song. However, the word also has a more general, if rarely used meaning which, simply stated, is the course of life on earth. Thus, rather than trying to figure out if anybody in "Pilgrimage" is off to a shrine, it's much easier to understand the changes of fortune described in the song as the usual experiences of life.

Of course, that's a pretty one-dimensional view of the song and doesn't take into account the appearance in the lyric of two-headed cows or of someone speaking in tongues. I'm unaware of the birth of any actual two-headed cows, except possibly near a nuclear power station, so such a creature's appearance in the song is presumably a symbol for bad luck.

Speaking in tongues usually does have a religious connotation, being the ability to speak in weird celestial languages brought on by divine ecstasy. Coupled, as it is in the song, with the words "it's worth a broken lip," makes the line suggestive of religious persecution. And the line "Take our fortune" could well indicate the acceptance of one's lot, good or bad—the bad, no doubt, including being persecuted for one's faith. It has also been suggested, taking into account both the cow and the tongues, that the song is about the relationship between superstition and religion, a relationship that traditionally has been very close in certain parts of the South.

While not wishing to deny the religious elements in the song (and Stipe has always been fond of including them) these images could just as easily be secular. Looking at it in another way then, "speaking in tongues" could refer to foreigners or indeed anybody who doesn't speak like you—anybody with a patois, an accent, or a vocabulary that's different. Consequently, there may well be two people or two groups of people addressed in the song: The haters, who believe that their bad luck (the two-headed cow) is entirely the fault of some other group identifiable by their "different" speech; and the hated, who are just trying to get on with their lives. "Pilgrimage," then, might very well be a song about intolerance.

Of course, as in most Stipe songs, there is an almost total lack of personal pronouns in "Pilgrimage," or, such as there are, they get switched around indiscriminately. This certainly makes it hard to differentiate individuals or groups within the song, let alone work out how they relate to each other. It's one of the many things that makes a Stipe lyric both frustrating and a challenge.

Thus, the fact that "Pilgrimage" might be about intolerance, or, indeed, the relationship between superstition and religion, must remain speculation. It doesn't help matters, of course, that the author later stated, "'Pilgrimage' still baffles me. At one point, right after we recorded it, I heard it and it made perfect sense. I was so exhilarated. I thought I had accomplished what I set out to do. And then I forgot!" And on another occasion he told a radio interviewer: "There are three points of view in the song, and I'm not sure which one the singer is taking yet."

"Moral Kiosk"	Not quite as discordant as "9-9," "Moral Kiosk" is another of R.E.M.'s slightly disturbing rockers. This one opens with Buck alone, playing an abrasive, repeated chord, and there is a decidedly choppy quality to the rhythm once the other two join in. The chorus section, musically, is one of their most distinctive, with Berry setting up a pounding drum pattern that sounds like bouncing boulders.

The chorus is highly effective, vocally, with Mike Mills practically chanting the harmony. On some live performances of the song, he would get really carried away, his voice taking on an extraordinary, plangent quality, matched perfectly by Stipe's quasi-yodeling.

Although there is some debate about the actual words of "Moral Kiosk," they are relatively clear and, aided by hints from the band, their overall subject matter is also relatively easy to grasp. In fact, with "Moral Kiosk," we even have some indication of Stipe's initial inspirations. The most commonly cited one refers to the existence of two poles on College Avenue in Athens, on which students and others place messages, advertisements for gigs, and philosophical diatribes. These two landmarks have been known for decades as the "moral kiosks."

Stipe's other starting point for the song is less well known. In the summer of 1983, shortly after *Murmur* was released, Stipe told a radio interviewer that the title related to the time he spent in Germany when he was seven. Apparently, while living there, he visited the castle of King Louis (I think he meant Ludwig, but never mind) and still had the brochure.

Unfortunately the interviewer didn't get him to elaborate, but it's possible to make a good stab at what he was talking about. The original meaning of "kiosk" was an open summerhouse or pavilion, the sort of thing to be found in the grounds of a castle. The intriguing question, of course, is whether the one Stipe saw, and still had information about in the brochure, was called the Moral Kiosk. It is just conceivable that Louis/Ludwig used the structure for philosophical or moral debates. Without a clearer answer from Stipe, or more details about the king in question, it's impossible to know.

As members of the band have said on various occasions, "Moral Kiosk" is about hypocrisy, particularly the kind perpetrated by any number of TV evangelists who prey on the weak-minded for money in the name of God, only to get caught with hookers in motel rooms. Needless to say, Stipe's words are not that prosaic. The song is obviously about hypocrisy, but there's no overt mention of TVs or hookers. It is a good lyric, though—one of Stipe's best in my opinion. It's full of rich imagery and deft poetic touches, such as the assonance in the first two lines: "Scratch the scandals in the twilight / Trying to shock, but instead idle hands all orient to her."

One line in "Moral Kiosk" does provide a sharp reminder of what can happen if you place too much emphasis on decoding individual words or phrases in Stipe's lyrics. The line in question is "She was laughing like a Horae." This line has had various Stipeologists racing to their encyclopedias of Greek myth, and yes, the Horae are in there. They are the goddesses of the seasons, daughters of Zeus and Themis, an interesting group of ladies, but there is nothing about them laughing.

The fact is that, although he probably does say "Horae" in the *Murmur* version of the song, its possible significance is somewhat undermined by the fact that he sang something different almost every time they did it live. These variants include "Horace," "Poet," "Whore," "Horse" (which actually does make sense idiomatically), "Hurry," (possibly "Hurricane," with the second syllable buried), and a noncommittal "Huhhh." Quite clearly, Stipe just chose whatever word or sound he felt like, and that word, per se, had no relevance to the song as a whole.

For whatever reason, "Moral Kiosk" remains one of the more underrated of R.E.M.'s songs. Maybe they just wrote so many good ones during this period it's inevitable that a few have been overlooked. Certainly it's a less obvious "classic" than, say, "Gardening at Night," "Laughing," or "Talk About the Passion." But, as an almost perfect marriage of powerful music and lyric imagery that is consistent throughout, "Moral Kiosk" is hard to beat.

"Perfect Circle"

"Perfect Circle" was written at about the same time as "Moral Kiosk," which is to say sometime around May or June of 1982; both were certainly being performed by the early part of July. There, however, the resemblance ends. "Perfect Circle" is virtually unique in the R.E.M. canon for several reasons, not least because it's one of only a handful where the band admits that one person alone wrote the music: Bill Berry.

To be strictly accurate, the song, as composed, was little more than an extended riff that Bill came up with in his kitchen on a little Casio keyboard. His intent, from its inception, was that "Perfect Circle" should be primarily performed on piano. The band loved the song and made a few attempts to play it onstage. As Bill later recalled: "I couldn't play drums and piano at the same time, so I had had this little toy Casio, which is what I wrote it on, and we would inevitably spill beer into it and stuff and the tempo would change, and it wouldn't work. So it kind of scared us off for a while."

The one place they could make it work was in the studio. As Mitch Easter told author Craig Rosen:

> We decided to make it bigger [than the aborted live version] and use the real pianos. It was Bill and Mike playing at the same time on these two different pianos that Reflection [studio] had. One was a real nice piano, the other was an old upright piano. The combination of the two together was a really nice sound. That's definitely the basis of that song.

The track was rounded out by some minimal drumming, presumably overdubbed by Berry; a bass part supplied by engineer Don Dixon; backward guitar courtesy of Easter; and some overdubbed acoustic guitars. Whether one of the latter was played by Buck is unknown. When asked about it in the early '90s, he had no recollection of playing on the track. He did admit, however, that the song was one of his favorites.

Stipe told me his opinion of "Perfect Circle" when I interviewed him in 1983: "When I hear that song I think—this is real cheesy—of *Romeo and Juliet*, the scene where they have the minstrels playing. It's kind of like a medieval-sounding melody. It just happened that way."

Although the tune is acknowledged as being Berry's, the lyrics were written by Stipe. Once again we have two different possible starting points for the words. The first comes from Buck, who, in 1984, recalled,

The most moving moment I've had in the last couple of years was at the end of one of our tours. I hadn't slept in days. I was as tired as I could possibly be, and we were doing a concert that night for a live radio show. And I was standing in the City Gardens in Trenton, New Jersey, at the back door, and it was just getting dark. These kids were playing touch football, the last game before dark came, and for some reason I was so moved I cried for twenty minutes. It sounds so trivial, but that's more or less what "Perfect

Michael searching for signs of the South.
(Photo by Laura Levine)

Circle" on *Murmur* is about. I told Michael to try and capture that feeling. There's no football in there, no kids, no twilight, but it's all there.

By contrast, Stipe, when asked about it in 1985, claimed that it was about his ex-girlfriend and denied any connection with "young boys playing baseball [sic]."

Despite Stipe's denial, the two explanations are not mutually exclusive. Buck claims it was the emotion of the situation that he wanted Stipe to capture. The emotional effect achieved in the song could easily reflect what Buck felt, even if the words bear little relation to what he actually saw.

Stipe's "ex-girlfriend" scenario does seems more relevant to the actual lyrics: there is clearly a romantic situation being described, even if the words, taken as a whole, are as enigmatic as ever. Nonetheless, some of the lines are quite literal descriptions of a postcoital interlude: "Put your hair up, we get to leave" and "Pull your dress on and stay real close." Others are less literal but still on the subject, like "Drink another, coin a phrase," which suggests a reflective glass of wine and intimate small talk.

Other lines are more mysterious. "Standing too soon, shoulders high in the room" sounds almost like the description of a baby learning to walk. Maybe the couple are taking their first adult steps? Alternatively, the narrator's lover has left the bed too quickly. If the disappointed narrator is still lying down, then the other's shoulders would appear "high in the room" and, yes, she would be "standing too soon."

"Heaven assumed" presumably means that they've had a very good time, as in "that was heaven." Granted, but it's still an odd use of the phrase. In Christian theology, only two individuals, Christ and the Virgin Mary, have ascended into heaven bodily, or to use the correct terminology, they were "assumed." I'm fairly certain that Stipe does not have messianic tendencies, but it is another fascinating use of a quasi-religious allusion. Then again, the couple might have "assumed" that what they were going to do would be heavenly, but in the event it wasn't. That's always good for a little postcoital angst and introspection, especially when young.

Most of the remaining lines are even more oblique. What is one to make of "Who might leave you where I left off? / A perfect circle of acquaintances and friends"? The second line on its own might just be a good play on words: it's common to speak of a "circle of friends," and if they are all good people one might see them as perfect. A perfect circle is also, of course, a geometric concept and in this case might mean nothing more than that friend A knows B who knows C who knows D who knows A.

Author Marcus Gray has suggested that the perfect circle has echoes of the cycle, or the circle, of life: in the song there are babies, Peter's footballing kids (the "shallow figure" and the "eleven shadows"), and the young postcoital adults, as well as intimations of death (the "eleven gallows"). Gray's idea, therefore, does makes sense.

Unfortunately, if the "perfect circle" line is intrinsically connected to the preceding one ("Who might leave you, where I left off?") as it appears to be, then "a perfect circle of acquaintances and friends" is the cynical answer to the question, and the narrator's lover is being passed around. Hopefully, the line doesn't really mean anything, because otherwise, the cynical version does undermine the tone and mood of the song.

Quibbles aside, there is no doubt that both lyrically and musically, "Perfect Circle" is perhaps the most achingly beautiful song R.E.M. have ever written. As Stipe so pithily described it, "It's a real gut-spiller."

"We Walk"

Written around July or August of '82, "We Walk" has been much reviled as being "overly sweet" and "twee." It has even been suggested that it was conceived as a joke. For my part, I've always enjoyed it, although nobody would seriously put it on an R.E.M. top-10 list. I would certainly concede that it is their most childlike song, and although it has been described as sounding like a nursery rhyme, I always felt that it had more of the quality of A. A. Milne's *Winnie The Pooh* stories. Musically, it has a faux-military feel to it, particularly in the drumming, but we are definitely talking about toy soldiers here, rather than the real thing.

Lyrically, "We Walk" is Stipe at his most minimal. Of the opening line, Stipe told me in 1983, "I used to know a girl who lived on the sec-

ond floor of this house and every time she walked up the stairs she would say, "Up the stairs into the hall." She didn't get a credit but I did say 'thank you.'" Her name was Dory Duke, and friends from the time still remember the two of them hanging out, with Dory usually walking a good five paces behind Stipe.

The phrase "Marat's bathing" refers to the death of the French Revolution martyr, Jean Paul Marat, murdered in his bath by Charlotte Corday. The image that Stipe obviously had in mind was Jacques-Louis David's striking 1793 painting of the subject. However, it seems Michael got the idea for the line—and possibly the "up the stairs" line—from the Print Shop in Athens. Stipe once told an audience (in relation to "We Walk") that if you walk up the stairs at the Print Shop, you have to walk through the bathroom in order to get to the kitchen. Apparently you would often see someone taking a bath "with their arm extended down over the edge, like that painting."

"We Walk" was never really taken very seriously by the band and often turned into an audience participation piece. There was the time, for example, when the band got the audience to shout, "eins, zwei, drei," at the end of the "into the hall" part, where Stipe would normally sing "oh, oh, oh." Hmm.

Arguably "7 Chinese Bros." shouldn't be included here. Although a good part of it was written and, indeed, performed before the end of 1982, it clearly wasn't complete enough to be realistically considered for inclusion on *Murmur*. As Buck later said, "We played that one for a year before we came up with a bridge. Every time we played it we'd just do a different bit of noise." In fact, Buck is indulging in a certain amount of hyperbole. By June of '83, if not before, the song was finished: bridge, words, and all— essentially the version that was recorded for *Reckoning*.

Superficially a slight throwback to their more "linear" folk-rockers, what "7 Chinese Bros." has in its favor, apart from a wonderful melody, is a real feeling of drama. Much of this is achieved by Stipe's vocal, which ranges from the *sotto voce* speaking of the verse to the full-throated, yet plaintive singing on the chorus.

The initial inspiration for the lyric was a 1938 children's story, "The Five Chinese Brothers," by Claire Huchet Bishop and Kurt Wiese. Stipe later claimed that " I got my facts wrong" when he added two extra brothers. Quite possible, of course, but it's just as likely that he thought two syllables fitted better than one. In any case, he certainly wasn't the only member of the band to have read the book. Mike Mills told *Blitz* in late 1984, "That story used to scare me as a child. The same goes for Michael. He adopted the children's tale to his current views of life, at the same time intending to evoke images of childhood."

In the end, Stipe only seems to have taken one image directly from the story, that of the "seven Chinese brothers swallowing the ocean"— although in the tale only one brother could do that. Nonetheless, in line with Mills's comment, much of the verse could easily be read as the memory of a childhood incident. Marcus Gray, in *It Crawled from the South,* suggests that the childhood memories in question might be the piano lessons taken by the young Stipe. Certainly it describes the meeting and presumably subsequent relationship of an adult and a child; references to a symphony and "the battle" (i.e., the lesson itself) could substantiate the claim. But, it's a little too vague to be sure.

The lines "Seven thousand years to sleep away the pain / She will return, she will return" allegedly refer to the death of Stipe's friend, the photographer Carol Levy, who took the cover photo for the band's first single. The song "Camera," also on *Reckoning*, is certainly about Levy, but, as far as I know, none of the band have ever said that the line in "7 Chinese Bros." also refers to her. Regardless, the lines have a pleasing echo of the "Once and Future King" idea. According to the legend, King Arthur merely sleeps and will return at the hour of his country's greatest need. This line, as sung by Stipe, especially when combined with Mills's harmony, is one of the most haunting parts of any R.E.M. song.

"Talk About the Passion"

Although everybody agrees that "Talk About the Passion" wasn't finished until the band was actually in the studio recording *Murmur*, there is a slight discrepancy over its composition date. According to Mitch Easter, "They had been playing it some, but they didn't have an arrangement. It was kind of rambling and went on forever. We kind of worked the arrangement out right then, and then recorded it. That was fun to do." However, members of the band have suggested that they'd never played it all the way through before they went into the studio, which is not quite the same thing.

Although the studio arrangement is more elaborate than what was later performed live, the basics remained the same: the delicate picked-guitar intro; the lovely melody; the definitive mournful, not to say passionate, Stipe vocal; and the first of what has always been a rare animal, a Buck guitar solo. As he told *Musician* shortly after the release of the album, "That was something Mike just taught me. I could probably have worked it out for myself, because I come up with things that are pretty much similar, but I thought it was really funny—my one little guitar solo, and the bass player came up with it."

Lyrically, "Talk About the Passion" is surprisingly straightforward, and as long as you have some knowledge of French ("Combien de temps?") the words are easy to decipher. It's also one of the songs whose meaning has been discussed by members of the band. One aspect of the song is religious hypocrisy, rather like "Moral Kiosk." Buck told *Melody Maker* in 1984, "People like Jerry Falwell are just Nazis. They're really evil, life-hating people, and Reagan is really aligned with it. A song like 'Talk About the Passion' is really rejecting that kind of fake religion." By contrast, Stipe told the *Los Angeles Times* in 1985: "When I wrote it, I was thinking about all the hunger in the world, which sounds like a cliché now,

"Skank" always included: "A series of crescendos that involved lots of feedback from Buck and Mills plus howling from Stipe." 930 Club, Washington, DC, March 12, 1983.
(PHOTO BY LAURA LEVINE)

[i.e., after Band Aid] but this was a year and a half ago." Both points of view can be read into the song. The line "Empty prayer, empty mouths" certainly includes both ideas.

The title itself is rich and multilayered. "Passion" literally means suffering, which ties in with Stipe's theme of hunger. But "Passion" is also used very specifically to speak of the events leading up to and including the crucifixion of Christ—which, when coupled with the next line, "Not everyone can carry the weight of the world," puts the song firmly in religious territory.

"Passion" can also refer to, as the dictionary puts it, "intense emotion, compelling action," with a nod toward sexual activity. This juxtaposition would not be the first or last time that Stipe seems to equate sexual and religious ecstasy.

TALKING ABOUT THE PASSION

R.E.M.: <u>MURMUR</u>

THREE

DASHT HOPES AT THE DRIVE-IN: THE EARLY RECORDING SESSIONS

Songs recorded: "Dangerous Times," "All the Right Friends," "Different Girl," "Narrator," "Just a Touch," "Baby I," "Mystery to Me," "Permanent Vacation"

The session held on July 6, 1980, at Wuxtry's Record Shop has caused all manner of confusion over the years, and even now the full story isn't totally clear. When a tape of it first appeared on the collectors' circuit in 1984, it was simply labeled, "Rehearsal Demos, 1980." Later it was dubbed "Atlanta Demos," and then "Tyrone's Demos, Autumn, 1980." The situation is still sufficiently confused for fans to talk about demos recorded on a four-track at Tyrone's in autumn, 1980, as separate from the Wuxtry tape when, in fact, they are one and the same. There are, of course, live tapes from Tyrone's dating from late 1980 and early 1981 that include otherwise unreleased R.E.M. songs; so there are genuine Tyrone's tapes, but they should not be confused with the Wuxtry tape.

The currently accepted lore states that the Wuxtry tape is, in fact, the partial soundtrack to a video made at a band practice session. The video was made by Mark Methe, owner of the chain of Wuxtry record stores, and one of his managers, Dan Wall. It wasn't, in fact, the first time they'd shot the band. An earlier attempt at Tyrone's, on May 5, had been largely a dis-

"Hi, I'm Michael."
(PHOTO BY LAURA LEVINE)

75

aster, marred by no sound and poor lighting. A practice session at one of the stores gave them the illusion, at least, of a little more control.

On the day of the Wuxtry shoot, R.E.M. were en route to the Warehouse in Atlanta, their first out-of-Athens gig, which is probably how the mistaken notion that the tapes were "Atlanta Demos" came about. One thing that isn't clear is how planned the shoot was. It's possible that the band stopped off in Decatur just to say hello, and the presence of the camera proved too tempting. In any event, they ran through their entire set on camera with the vague intention of selecting one song to be used as a promo clip to secure more gigs.

For whatever reason the project was not pursued; however, nearly three years later, Methe decided to make use of some of the material. As he told Denise Sullivan, author of *Talk About the Passion*, "Some hip-pretending weasel made a bootleg of the cassette I made when R.E.M. rehearsed at Wuxtry. I duplicated it cheaply on real lo-fi and gave them away to people I deemed to be fans. I never thought someone was going to make a bootleg."

Most fans, of course, remain unmoved by Methe's moral indignation and consider that he did them a favor. Even if the tapes lack any kind of production values and sounded really murky by the time most people heard them, their historical interest is undeniable. The performance of the songs is full of energy, but the songs themselves are largely inept, with only "Just a Taste" showing anything like the promise of the band's post-summer 1980 material. Nonetheless, hearing, or even better, seeing the whole session would be fascinating. But nothing else from it has ever passed into general circulation.

Bombay Studio, Smyrna, Georgia, February 8, 1981

Tracks recorded: "Sitting Still," "Gardening at Night," "Radio Free Europe," "Shaking Through," "Mystery to Me," "(Don't Go Back to) Rockville," "Narrator," "White Tornado"

Until the early '90s, this session was even more of a mystery than the Wuxtry session and was frequently confused with it. When I interviewed Buck in late 1983, he told me: "Well, we had made probably one of the world's worst demo tapes ever, at an eight-track studio in Atlanta. No fault of the guy who taped it, we just didn't know what we were doing, and we went in and did seven songs in two hours."

R.E.M.: <u>MURMUR</u>

At that point I hadn't heard any of the demos. However, during the course of writing my resulting R.E.M. piece, I acquired a copy of the "1980 Demos" and made the erroneous assumption that it was the same tape that Buck had been talking about. The confusion lasted for many years, probably because no other tape fitting the description ever came to light. Finally, word got out of the Bombay session, but until author Marcus Gray tracked down Joe Perry, Bombay's owner, there was no information available about it.

The background to the session proved to be relatively straightforward. In the fall of 1980 the band took on Jefferson Holt, a friend from North Carolina, first as roadie and then manager. One of his first recommendations was that they needed to make a good demo tape, one that included their new-style songs like "Gardening at Night." The band agreed, with the stipulations, at least from Buck, that any studio they chose should be cheap, good, and close to Athens, and that whoever produced the session should have some understanding of the band's music. After sounding out his various contacts, Holt came up with Joe Perry at Bombay studios.

Perry is an interesting guy. By the time he was sixteen he was playing in bands, and more to the point, he was already collecting recording equipment. In the late '70s, and still only in his late teens, he realized that he had enough hardware to open a studio. He found premises in Smyrna, near Atlanta, and opened Bombay. The name was chosen purely because he liked it, but in short order he decked out the lobby with clay elephants and pictures of India.

Partly through economic necessity and partly through choice, Bombay was only an eight-track facility. Nonetheless, it rapidly acquired a good reputation. As Perry recalled: "Although Bombay was small, it was known for its live ambient sound. . . . I used no digital effects; all the sounds of the studio were created with special miking techniques."

Perry himself also became popular, not only because he was a quick-witted producer, engineer, and mixer, but because he was sympathetic to young rock bands. Unlike most of the other local studios, he imposed no rules on them when it came to recording, particularly in regard to volume.

R.E.M. arrived at Bombay with a short list of songs they wanted to record. Their selection was interesting: four songs, "Radio Free

Europe," "Sitting Still," "Shaking Through," and "Gardening at Night," must have almost selected themselves, because they were far and away the best songs R.E.M. had yet written. "Rockville" was a little more marginal, but even in its original speedy version was a classy pop song. Of the remaining three, "White Tornado" was understandable; the band had only just written it, and as a campy instrumental, it at least demonstrated another facet of their music. The other two, "Mystery to Me" and "Narrator," are a little harder to fathom. Although they are both marginally superior to some of the other songs they'd written prior to "Gardening at Night," they were certainly not equal to more recent efforts like "Just a Touch" or "Windout." Indeed, as hard-edged rockers, either of those latter two would have further demonstrated their versatility.

In any event, the band spent the best part of a day recording their chosen tracks, considerably longer, of course, than the two hours that Buck, ever the master of myth and hyperbole, later claimed they'd taken.

To what extent the band followed Perry's suggestions is not known, but the way the songs were recorded probably pleased both parties. On each song, seven of the eight tracks were used up simultaneously with the band playing live. The extra track was then available for overdubs but was only used on three songs: extra backing vocals on "Sitting Still," a guitar overdub on "Radio Free Europe," and guitar fills on "Narrator." According to Perry, "They didn't know much about recording, but they were able to get the energy across on tape." His final verdict about the tapes was that they were (and remain) really hot, and he was consequently surprised, therefore, when R.E.M. did nothing with them.

Originally, the band had hoped to use these tapes in two ways. Ideally, they hoped to take two of the tracks and issue them as a single. However, whether they felt these recordings were good enough to merit release was a moot point. According to Perry, neither he nor the band could afford to put out a record. The other plan for this session was to use all or part of it as promotional material, to send tapes to record companies, and to secure gigs. Reasonable expectations for the quality of a tape made for those purposes would be somewhat lower than of a tape meant to be released. Even so, the band did nothing with these recordings. On the face of it, this seems a considerable waste of time, effort, and money. And although Perry may be a little biased, his assessment of the tapes is not that far off the mark. He was later told that the band had been unhappy with the backing vocals. But even if that's true, it would have been a very easy problem to fix.

It's doubtful that the Bombay sessions contain any great revelations, but since none of the tracks have passed into circulation, it's impossible to say for sure. In any case, all of the tracks were rerecorded at various times, some more than once, and all except "Mystery to Me" have been officially issued.

The band's curious attitude toward the Bombay tapes was possibly summed up by Mike Mills, who told the *Atlanta Journal* around the time of the session, "What we want to do is make one single or demo tape that's the most killer thing ever done, then we'll die in a car wreck or plane crash." Mills's attitude, while flippant and redolent of a fear of failure, was probably true in one respect: It's quite likely that the band had no real reason to expect commercial success. On the indie circuit of the time, just about the best you could hope for was a well-received tape or single. On that basis, if whatever they recorded was going to be their swan song, rather than the next step in their evolution, it would have to be really good rather than just acceptable. And Perry's enthusiasm notwithstanding, the Bombay tape may simply not have been it.

Buck later claimed that Holt was particularly unhappy with this tape. He said that Holt told them: "This tape is really horrible, I really don't want to send it around, because, if anything, it's going to scare people off hiring you guys." However, given Buck's tendency to color past events from his own perspective, it's difficult to know if this is true.

Whatever the truth of the matter, the upshot was that Holt began casting around for another studio. As Buck told me in 1983, "[Holt] called up Peter Holsapple of the dB's, who was a mutual friend from Chapel Hill, North Carolina, and said, 'Who's cheap and easy to work with and isn't going to be a real jerk?' And he said, 'Mitch' [Easter]. We didn't know who he was but we said, 'OK, fine.'"

Despite being only a little older than R.E.M.'s senior member, Peter Buck, Holsapple and Easter had been stalwarts of the Chapel Hill/Winston-Salem scene for years. In fact, Easter joined his first band, The Loyal Opposition, in 1968, when he was a mere twelve years old. For the next decade he played in a series of bands including Sacred Irony, Rittenhouse Square, and the Sneakers, all of which, at various times, included Holsapple and the other future dB's frontman, Chris Stamey.

Although they sometimes recorded, these bands never achieved much success, even locally. This was largely because they favored the music of the British Invasion bands, especially the Move, in an era when most North Carolinians preferred heavy metal.

When punk hit in 1976, Stamey moved up to New York and formed a band with his hero, ex-Big Star member Alex Chilton. When that band folded, Stamey formed the dB's with two other transplanted Winston-Salemites, Will Rigby and Gene Holder, the trio swelling to a quartet when Holsapple finally joined in October 1978. Both Stamey and Holsapple wrote excellent punk-tinged pop songs and the dB's quickly acquired a reputation in New York as one of the premier New Wave bands.

After Stamey moved up to New York, Easter worked with Holsapple in a new band, the H-Bombs. Although they played live, most of the time the H-Bombs, or rather Holsapple and Easter, simply made tapes. At these sessions, even though Easter could play guitar, sax, drums, and cello, Holsapple did most of the playing; Easter concentrated on the tape machine. It was purely amateur stuff done in their respective homes, but it gave Easter a taste for production. When Holsapple moved up to New York in late '78, Easter raised the money to buy proper studio equipment. Eighteen months or so later, he opened the sixteen-track Drive-In Studios in the garage of his parents' home in Winston-Salem. One of the studio's first jobs was to mix part of the dB's first album.

Although R.E.M. was unaware of Mitch Easter, they were big fans of the dB's, which is presumably why they were happy to accept Holsapple's recommendation. Holsapple didn't, of course, vanish from R.E.M.'s life at that point. In October 1982, he opened for R.E.M. as a solo act (the dB's were temporarily inactive), usually joining them onstage for the encores. Almost two years later, the full dB's acted as the support band for a three-week leg of R.E.M.'s Little America tour, and in 1989 Holsapple actually became a temporary fifth member of R.E.M. for the Green world tour. He repeated this role, albeit in the guise of Spanish Charlie, on 1991's pseudonymous Bingo Hand Job tour.

Songs recorded: "Radio Free Europe," "Sitting Still," "White Tornado," plus various snippets

R.E.M.'s first encounter with Mitch Easter took place on April 15, 1981, just two days after Jefferson Holt had talked to him on the phone. Apparently Easter had heard of R.E.M. or, at least, had seen a poster of them. But as he later recalled: "I had this really strong image [that] they were a high-tech band with synths and a drum machine."

It didn't take Easter long to discover his mistake and, from the first, he found the members of R.E.M. really easy to get along with. For its part, the band was almost astonished at how easygoing things were at Drive-In. In later interviews, Buck was prone to getting carried away about the place, particularly about Easter's mother who, he claimed, would serve food and coffee at 3 A.M. Mitch later attempted to tone down this rosy vision: "I don't think she was quite the ultimate TV mom. It wasn't that cute, but it was a really good atmosphere."

Probably as a result of feeling that they'd squeezed too many songs into their one-day Bombay session, the band wisely limited themselves to three on that first day with Easter, a number they could complete in the short amount of time they had available. Also, although no doubt pleased with the flexibility afforded by working with sixteen-track equipment, the band made little use of the extra tracks on this first visit. Nor, indeed, did they take the opportunity to experiment very much. The sound on the tapes, barring a few overdubs of extra guitar parts and backing vocals, is very much the live R.E.M. sound, which, at the time, is just what they wanted.

Stipe's vocals were another matter. He chose to sing at the far end of the room, facing the wall, in order to make his voice as unintelligible as possible, particularly on "Radio Free Europe." He later claimed that he did it because he hadn't written any words to "Radio Free Europe" at that point, so it was all nonsense. But, in fact, you can make out the words, strange though they may be, and Mitch Easter still has Stipe's lyric sheet from the session. Not only are the words on the sheet pretty much the same as he sings on the record, they're also virtually the same as the ones later reprinted in *Song Hits*—the ones Stipe claimed he'd made up for the magazine as a joke.

Shortly after the session, the band put together a fun, but decidedly low-tech, cassette package that was duly sent out. The first 300 or so contained mixes of the three completed songs, "Radio Free Europe," "Sitting Still," and "White Tornado." However, as Buck told *Goldmine* in 1987, it also included "about ten seconds of 'Sitting Still,' done polka-style and about half of this surf song where it stops in the middle and I go 'Whoops, I fucked up.'" There was a second version produced of about a hundred copies that also contained another Easter mix of "Radio Free Europe," a deliberately amateur and very funny attempt to re-create the dub mixes found on Jamaican reggae records.

The packaging was also a tad eccentric for a promotional device. As an insert, they included cut-up baseball-card size photos of the band and then sealed each of them with a label stating, "Danger—Do Not Open!" Fortunately most people ignored the warning. The band sent them to just about everybody they could think of: record companies, clubs, magazines (including *Women's Wear Daily*), family, and friends. For a first offering from an unknown band from somewhere other than the big metropolitan areas, the tape did its job surprisingly well. Both *New York Rocker* and the *Village Voice* gave it glowing reviews, and they received several inquiries from record companies, including a few they hadn't sent the tape to! According to R.E.M. legend, they threw all such letters away.

The initial batch of tapes was sent out at the end of May, primarily to the New York media, in time for the band's first appearances in the city in early June. At about the same time the tapes went out, the band went back to Drive-In—but not to record new material.

The dB's c. 1982. *Left to right:* Will Rigby, Peter Holsapple, Chris Stamey, Gene Holder. (PHOTO FROM THE AUTHOR'S COLLECTION)

Remix of "Radio Free Europe"

Accounts vary as to what happened in the weeks following the April Drive-In session, but one thing that remains undisputed is that the band was approached by Atlanta-based ex-musician Jonny Hibbert, who was on the verge of starting his own independent label, Hib-Tone Records. He volunteered to make R.E.M. the first band on the label and to release a single of "Radio Free Europe" and "Sitting Still," using the tapes they'd already done at Drive-In. The band, desperate to release something and attracted by the fact that Hib-Tone would become an Athens label, agreed. Unfortunately Hibbert insisted on two conditions: first, that they should remix "Radio Free Europe," with Hibbert as executive producer,

Drive-In Studios, Winston-Salem, NC, May 25, 1981

and second, that he would retain the publishing rights. They agreed to both, a decision they would come to regret. The band's friend and lawyer Bertis Downs partially renegotiated the record deal, shortening it to six months with no options, but the other parts of the deal, the publishing and the remixing, stood.

Hibbert argues to this day that his decision to remix was not borne out of ego. As he told author Denise Sullivan,

> We got the rough mixes of stuff they had done at Mitch's Drive-In Studio and went back up there. . . . I wanted R.E.M. to sound the way they sounded when I first heard them in Tyrone's. We got the best mix we could at that point and left Mitch's. Later Mitch did another mix on his own of the same stuff and said he thought it was an improvement on the first mix. Peter was the most vocal in wanting to use Mitch's new mix, but I put my foot down, and we released the mix I preferred. I was probably the last person to override Pete Buck.

Not surprisingly, Mitch still prefers his second mix (third, if you include the dub mix), which was ultimately used on the *Eponymous* compilation album. He also thinks, and he's probably right, that all three are pretty similar. In his sleeve notes to *Eponymous*, Buck mentions something called the "cattle call mix" that he claims is available on bootlegs. Since no further mixes have surfaced, my guess is that he's referring to the dub mix.

The controversy didn't end with the single's mix, unfortunately. When the band received copies of the finished record, they were bitterly disappointed, particularly Buck, who ceremoniously broke a copy and taped it to his wall. To this day no one is really sure whether the problem was the mix, the mastering, the pressing, or any combination of the three. Certainly the record is pretty muddy-sounding, but that didn't stop it doing surprisingly well, and it ended up on the end-of-year top-10 lists of several critics. With further disputes over the number of records pressed and sold, there was no way the band were going to work with Hibbert again. They were back on their own.

They still believed that, despite the alleged overtures, no major label would really sign them, nor would they wish to be on a major. The only label they professed any interest in was IRS, whose championing of the Police and left-field American bands like the Cramps appealed to R.E.M. In fact, via Berry's and Mills's old friend, Ian Copeland, brother of IRS head Miles, attempts were being made to get them on that label. However, because nothing seemed to be moving in that direction, R.E.M. fell back on the independent production/self-distribution approach.

At this point, the summer of 1981, they met David Healey, who has been described as either a wealthy art student from Princeton University or an old friend of Jefferson Holt from Chapel Hill. Because the two descriptions are not mutually exclusive, he could easily have been both. The band had played at the Princeton Summer Ball in June '81, so it's quite feasible that they got the gig because of Holt's friendship with Healey, and that they met Healey at the show.

In any event, Healey was so enthralled with the band that by the end of the summer he'd moved to Athens. The plan was that he would finance a new production company-cum-record label jointly controlled by him and the band, or at least Jefferson Holt. Healey, unlike Hibbert, certainly had the money, and because he was now a close and trusted friend, the band agreed. The company was to be called Dasht Hopes. Convinced of their own abilities and that their bills would be paid, a thoroughly confident R.E.M. re-entered Drive-In Studios to start work on a proposed EP.

Songs recorded: "1,000,000," "Ages of You," "Gardening at Night," "Carnival of Sorts (Box Cars)," "Stumble," "Shaking Through," "Jazz Lips," plus "9-9" attempted, but abandoned

Drive-In
Studios,
Winston-
Salem, NC,
October 2-4
and 7, 1981

While it's generally assumed that Mitch Easter and Drive-In had become R.E.M.'s natural first choice for producer and studio, this turns out not to be the case. Apparently the band had been considering a new studio near Atlanta, and word of this had reached Easter. He clearly remembers lobbying Jefferson Holt at a gig in Greensboro, telling him that the Hib-Tone single didn't represent the sound they could get and how they could do much better. Basically, he really liked the band and their music and wanted to work with them again. Also, and this is by no means a criticism, he probably realized that R.E.M., sooner or later, were going to become popular, and working with them would be no bad thing for him or the studio. From Holt's point of view, although he no doubt liked Drive-In's atmosphere as much as the band, I'm sure he also liked Easter's rates of $250 a day—a bargain at the time.

Although R.E.M. had a lengthy wish list of songs they wanted to record, having four days to work meant that, for the first time, they could actually give some thought to the sounds they wanted to achieve. According to Easter: "The band was ready to do cool stuff and stretch out a little." They still, however, knew next to nothing about how most affects were achieved. Buck remembers a conversation with Easter: "I was basically asking Mitch, 'What's this?' One day I asked what a tape loop was. So he made a tape loop, and we made a track and it took like an hour."

For Easter, almost all of it was fun. As he later recalled: "Some of the stuff I look back at fondly from those sessions was real normal studio stuff that was new to them and they thought was great. There was not much messing around with arrangements—they had the arrangements very well worked out, and I liked 'em, so we didn't do that. But when it came around to, 'Let's put more guitars on, let's have this backward tape loop,' and stuff, I think I had a lot to do with that. It was sort of kids with a new toy."

The band loved it, and it was a real learning process for them. As Buck told me in 1983, "So we went back to Mitch's place and recorded a bunch of songs consciously to put out our own record but also to experiment and learn how to use studios. . . . Every trick we'd ever heard of, we wanted to try to learn how to do it. So 'backward guitars? Sure. Let's go out and tape crickets and synch them in time.' All kinds of kitchen utensils used as percussion instruments, and dogs barking in the mix." Then, of course, there were Stipe's vocals. In 1991 Stipe recalled: "The entire *Chronic Town* sessions I spent with a trash can on my head, because somehow or other Mitch and I decided that it would be a great way to get a different acoustic sound to a vocal."

Most of the songs include innovative ideas. "Gardening at Night" features Easter's old Danelectro sitar. As Easter recalled: "It's a guitar with a bridge that's meant to buzz, and I've had that thing since the early seventies. . . . It sounds great."

The band ended up doing two mixes of "Gardening at Night" that are sufficiently different to be regarded as separate versions. The first features up-front acoustic guitars and a harsh, open-throated, Stipe vocal. The second has the overdubbed sitar and a soft Stipe vocal. This second version was chosen for the EP—although not without considerable debate within the band. The alternate mix was offered to, and rejected by, *Trouser Press* for them to release as a flexidisc, and was finally released on *Eponymous*.

The guitar parts on "Stumble" are both played by Peter, and both parts are the same except that one of them is played on a 12-string and makes use of a tremolo. "Stumble" also employs tape loops—a technique taken to its illogical conclusion on the infamous "Jazz Lips." Oh yes, and at the beginning of "Stumble" you can apparently hear what is allegedly Stipe, unzipping and zipping his fly. Hmm.

"Jazz Lips" was their masterpiece of self-indulgence. Buck described the track to me in 1983:

> One night when we were drunk, we did a ten-minute noise tape that was partially me making guitar feedback and then synching a drum tape [actually looped by Easter from part of the drum track for "1,000,000"] and chanting over the top, like Hawaiian chants. Michael was reading from some *Playboy*, or something like that [actually it was a story from *Cavalier* called "Jazz Lips"] from 1957, so you could hear all these neo-Bohemian phrases over the top. It was really bad—just for fun though. We wanted to see how to do looping and things like that, like George Clinton, except that it's not anywhere near as commercial or anything.

Needless to say, it has never been released.

There is one mystery about the "Jazz Lips" session. I have in my possession a photocopy of a log-sheet from Drive-In Studios for the day that R.E.M. recorded "Jazz Lips." From it one can discover that tracks one and two were a "normal loop," tracks three and four were a "low loop," tracks five and six were a "high loop," and tracks seven and eight were a "drum loop." The other three tracks were given over to "guitar" and "singing." The only problem is that the sheet is dated March 3, 1981, i.e., over a month before the Hib-Tone session, which was supposedly

their first visit to the studio. I spoke to Mitch Easter about it and he is as baffled as I am. Apart from anything else, as noted, the drum loop was made from Berry's drum part from "1,000,000," which was definitely recorded at the October 1981 sessions. Mitch is tickled by the possibility that someone might have forged the document, but neither of us could imagine who would do it or why they would bother. He still believes that "Jazz Lips" was cut in October 1981, and I'll go with that.

The other tracks feature less in the way of studio trickery, except for double-tracking and the occasional overdubbing of other instruments, such as the organ (or possibly guitar played through a Leslie speaker) buried deep in the mix of "Shaking Through." It should be noted that when asked about it in the early '90s, Easter had no recollection of a Drive-In recording of "Shaking Through." However, because it features the "early" lyrics, it's unlikely to be a *Murmur* outtake. And it certainly wasn't part of the Bombay or RCA sessions, a fact confirmed by the studio logs. The logical conclusion is that Mitch's memory was faulty. In any case, Buck had mentioned to me in 1983 that a version existed when we were discussing *Chronic Town* outtakes.

There are, however, yet more sources of confusion regarding the October '81 tapes. Over the years, there has been much debate about whether a second version of "White Tornado" was cut at the October Drive-In session. Informed opinion now favors the two-version theory, with the later version only available on bootleg. Three versions of "1,000,000" do exist, but close inspection reveals that they are just different mixes, and not nearly as different from each other as the two versions of "Gardening at Night."

Lastly, "9-9" was attempted, but according to Mitch remained unfinished because it was a new song that hadn't been properly worked out—although it has to be said that they'd been playing it on and off since the previous spring.

Despite having six finished songs in the can (seven, if you include "White Tornado," which had been used only on the cassette set), R.E.M. was obviously not satisfied and arranged another visit to Drive-In the following January.

**Songs recorded: "Wolves, Lower," "Carnival of Sorts (Box Cars),"
plus "Catapult" attempted, but never finished**

Drive-In
Studios,
Winston-
Salem, NC,
January 27
and 28,
1982

Why they didn't attempt "Wolves, Lower" at the October session is another mystery. In any case, this January '81 version is not the one used on the EP. As Easter explained to Craig Rosen, "We recorded it when we did the original batch of songs for the EP [not quite true] but it was fast as hell. The fast version even got mastered for vinyl, but then the band had second thoughts about the track."

The January "Carnival of Sorts" is usually regarded as a completely new recording, but I'm not so sure. Certainly they remixed it to great effect, and it probably has a new vocal, but I suspect that the basic track is the one from the previous October. The major addition is the fairground organ intro. Because they obviously couldn't afford to hire the real thing, they improvised. As Easter later recalled: "It was one of those [Casio keyboards] you can get for $30 at a department store. We used this old tape recorder microphone to mike that thing up to make it sound sort of bad and distant."

As with "9-9," "Catapult" was attempted, but never finished. This time they really did have the excuse that it was a new song.

Although they were theoretically committed to the Dasht Hopes project through the latter part of 1981, R.E.M. was still happy to follow up other leads, or at least to have others do it on their behalf. Thanks in part to the glowing reviews in the *Village Voice* and *New York Rocker*, the band had become minor celebrities in New York, at least among the cognoscenti. One of these was promoter Jim Fouratt. He'd been so impressed with the Hib-Tone single that he'd traveled to Athens in late '81 to see the band.

At the time, Fouratt was setting up a production company in New York with producer Kurt Monkacsi, who had worked (as he still does) with composer Philip Glass. Their idea, not exactly novel, was to record new bands and either license the masters to an existing record label or sign the band to a label or preferably both. Fouratt considered R.E.M. an ideal candidate for their first venture. By coincidence, Monkacsi was dating the head of A&R at RCA, Nancy Jeffries, who, among other things, had been lead singer in the Insect Trust, a New York-based late-'60s rock band. Thanks to this connection, Fouratt and Monkacsi secured free time at RCA's New York studio the following February for an R.E.M. session. The aim, of course, was to get the band signed to RCA.

RCA Studio C, New York, NY, February 1, 2, and 8, 1982

Songs recorded: "Catapult," "Wolves, Lower," "Laughing," "Romance," "Shaking Through," "Carnival of Sorts (Box Cars)," "Stumble"

In many ways the RCA sessions seem out of place in R.E.M.'s evolution. The band were still, theoretically, committed to the Dasht Hopes project; they had vowed never to sign with a major label, especially one whose chief output was Elvis Presley reissues. The idea of them working, through choice, with an unknown producer in a studio where the producer's mom was not on hand to provide midnight snacks, seems, at the very least, out of character. Of course, there are several reasons why they would have wanted to do it. Any interest from a major label must have been flattering, irrespective of their much-touted views on the subject, and free time in a 24-track studio in the Big Apple was not to be sneezed at.

A more basic reason may have been that their commitment to Dasht Hopes in general, and David Healey in particular, had been waning, and they were wisely attempting to keep their options open. As Buck told

R.E.M.: MURMUR

R.E.M. archivist Gary Nabors, "When we were doing *Chronic Town*, he [Healey] was supposed to be paying for it and we'd call up and go, 'Our van broke down, we're stranded.' and he'd go, 'Fuck you, I'm not going to pay the bill.' And hang up on us. . . . He was, like, a talker, you know? Like he almost got Keith Richards to give him five thousand dollars. He was a good friend, but it was totally crazy. He'd have these breakdowns." How much of this can be put down to post-facto justification of what eventually happened is debatable. Clearly though, all was not well with Dasht Hopes.

The RCA recordings themselves are also something of an aberration. If nothing else, they are quite unlike anything R.E.M. had done at Drive-In. There are no tape loops, backward guitar, or spoken sections on the RCA tapes. Clearly, Monkacsi didn't want to present the record company with anything overly complex or weird.

R.E.M. have rarely commented on the RCA sessions, although Buck did tell a radio interviewer in 1983: "We banged out seven songs in 15 hours at RCA. It didn't come out the way it should." Leaving aside Buck's usual hyperbole with regard to time (they were there for the best part of three days), the question is: From the band's point of view, how should the tapes have come out? One assumes that both parties had discussed up front what sort of sound they were going for, and R.E.M. must have realized that with Mokacsi at the controls, they were going to lose most of what Marcus Gray has called "their spooky otherness." Monkacsi presumably got what he wanted: a clean-sounding, professional tape with up-front vocals and an overall commercial sound.

Even knowing what to expect, maybe the band simply felt that the tapes were just not that hot. This is probably true, but the RCA tapes are not without interest. To start with, they include the first complete recordings of two more *Murmur* songs, "Laughing" and "Catapult"—although the latter was obviously still giving them problems because it took five takes of the basic track to get it right. The marginal but interesting "Romance" is given its first outing in the studio, and Mike Mills adds piano for the first time, notably on "Shaking Through." It was this piano addition, repeated on the *Murmur* version of the song that, in my opinion, raises the arrangement from a good to an excellent one. Overall, the RCA tapes provide an interesting insight into what R.E.M. might have sounded like if they had signed with RCA—or any other major label, for that matter.

Not surprisingly, none of the RCA tracks has ever been officially released. All of them, however, have surfaced on bootlegs. Although most collectors manage to sort them out, the RCA cuts that appear on bootlegs have always been misidentified. Usually they are mixed up indiscriminately with Drive-In outtakes, and all of them are referred to as either *Chronic Town* outtakes, IRS demos, or some variant thereof.

Identifying the RCA tracks is relatively straightforward. Aside from the versions released on *Murmur*, the RCA tapes contain the only available studio versions of "Laughing" and "Catapult," and, as noted, none of the RCA tracks contain extra effects. Also, presumably as a result of nervousness, all the songs are played at a much faster tempo than any of their other studio recordings.

One of the things all parties knew, in relation to RCA, was that they would take their time in making a decision about signing the band. Consequently, rather than hang around any longer, R.E.M. decided to carry on, for the time being, with Dasht Hopes. The story, however, does get a little confused here. Not in dispute is that sometime in the weeks following the RCA sessions, the band returned to Drive-In to add a few final overdubs and to mix their EP. Pleased with the results, Mitch Easter was dispatched on March 9 to Sterling Sound in New York City to master the record. What Easter worked on that day is not entirely clear. Certainly he mastered "1,000,000," "Gardening at Night," (sitar/soft vocal version), "Stumble," "Wolves, Lower," and the new version/remix of "Carnival of Sorts," from January '82. Whether he also mastered "Ages of You" and the acoustic version of "Gardening at Night" is open to question.

What is also in question is whether, by this stage, the recording was still a Dasht Hopes project. Certainly it's at this juncture that IRS reenters the picture. Apparently, Ian Copeland had tried to interest his brother Miles in signing R.E.M. back in June '81, but Miles had rejected the idea, assuming that his brother was simply trying to do a favor for some old friends.

Later in the year Mark Williams, an Atlanta DJ and a rep for A&M (IRS's distributor), had received and liked the Hib-Tone single. He sent it on to Jay Boberg, IRS's vice president on the West Coast, who liked the record, but did nothing more about it. Williams still had faith that Boberg could be won over and suggested to Jefferson Holt that he send Boberg any new tapes, as and when they were ready.

This is precisely what Holt did, sending Boberg a cassette of the Drive-In tapes at some point after they had been mixed back in February. This time Boberg was impressed and contacted Holt to tell him so. During the conversation, Boberg discovered that the band would be playing in New Orleans on March 12. Because Boberg was already planning to visit his girlfriend who lived there, he decided to see her and the band at the same time. The New Orleans show was a disaster, but by then Boberg was a convert and offered the band a deal with IRS the next day.

The only real question relating to the period of Boberg's initial interest in the band is how much Healey knew about it or, indeed, if he were still involved at all. One version of the story claims that Healey still expected the EP to be released on Dasht Hopes and, consequently, paid for the New York mastering.

By contrast, Mitch Easter claims that Healey was already out of the picture by early March. The mastering was only done, presumably, because Holt had sufficient faith that Boberg would indeed sign the band, and Holt was therefore prepared to make the necessary investment

Jefferson Holt and Sandra Lee-Phipps aboard the subway in New York, November 1982.
(PHOTO BY SANDRA LEE-PHIPPS)

required to send Mitch to Sterling Sound in New York. Since it transpired that Boberg couldn't actually sign the band without Miles Copeland's okay, the existence of finished masters may have helped to make the deal more attractive to IRS. This ploy makes sense when you know that the band were only willing to sign on the condition that IRS release the EP as it stood, rather than making them start again from scratch—the idea being that, with the mastering done, all that IRS would pay for was production and distribution.

If that was the case, R.E.M. made a smart move, because it turned out that IRS had reservations about the tapes. As Buck told me in 1983, "[Boberg] wasn't convinced that it [*Chronic Town*] was a great first record, but we said that it was part of the deal, because we didn't want to spend eight months putting out an album a year from then—we wanted something out fast."

To a large extent, the background to the IRS deal is only of academic interest. What matters is that on May 31, 1982, R.E.M. signed with the label. It is tempting to speculate, though, what would have happened if IRS had held out and refused to issue *Chronic Town*. One wonders which tracks from the EP would have ended up being rerecorded for *Murmur* and which *Murmur* tracks would have been bumped as a result. There is, of course, no way of knowing the answer to that question.

Whether or not Healey had paid for the New York mastering of the *Chronic Town* tapes, Dasht Hopes was now completely out of the picture. Healey promptly left Athens, feeling betrayed and disappointed. Fouratt and Monkacsi were also dropped, apparently just before RCA was finally about to make an offer. The other lingering problem was Jonny Hibbert. Although he couldn't reissue the Hib-Tone single himself, he still controlled the publishing on the two songs. Should the band rerecord the songs or reissue the tracks, he would continue to make a healthy income, provided he paid R.E.M. their royalties. The situation did not sit well with the band, who made it plain that they would never do anything with the songs as long as he controlled the publishing rights. It became clear to Hibbert that if he didn't sell back the rights, he would be branded in the industry as someone who didn't play fair. Short of money, he finally accepted an offer of $2,000. R.E.M. now owned all of their songs again. They were also going to have a record released that finally represented what they were about. Well, almost. On the day after signing with IRS, the band went back to Drive-In for one last recording session for the EP.

Song recorded: "Wolves, Lower" (slow version)

Drive-In
Studios,
Winston-
Salem, NC,
June 1,
1982

At some point, R.E.M. decided that the January version of "Wolves, Lower" was way too fast and that it needed to be redone. Although it's not known when that decision was made, the fact that they didn't go back to Drive-In until signing with IRS has to be significant. It's possible that part of their deal with IRS included the label's paying for a day at Drive-In, along with any subsequent work done on the resulting tape. It's more likely though that the band were footing the bill themselves; consequently, it seems reasonable that they only went back to the studio when they were safe in the knowledge that they had a record deal.

The new version of "Wolves, Lower" is not only slower, it's a great deal stronger. It also contains one of the more bizarre recording effects used on a rock record. Taking advantage of the early summer weather, Mitch Easter decided to tape the chorus outdoors. As he later recalled, "We had really loud insect noises there in good weather. . . . There's actually crickets buzzing under the vocals, which you don't really hear, but I think subliminally it must do something."

The band were finally satisfied that the tapes were as good as they were going to get, and the EP, now entitled *Chronic Town* (after a line from "Carnival of Sorts"), was released at the end of August 1982, to generally favorable reviews. If it has a fault, it's probably the production, which is a tad low-tech. And while one can admire the spirit of adventure shown by both the band and Easter, the studio effects may be just a little excessive.

The song selection is interesting. Why those five songs in particular? While there is a very good chance that they simply chose what they thought was their best material, there is a vague thematic link between four of the songs. "Gardening at Night," "1,000,000," "Stumble," and "Wolves, Lower" are all set, in whole or in part, in gardens or graveyards. Also, although it's specified only in "Gardening at Night" and the spoken section of "Stumble," there is a definite nocturnal feel to all of the songs.

There is also a pervading feeling of claustrophobia, but as much as anything that probably comes from the intentional production effects.

Mitch Easter at his Drive-In Studios.
(Photo by Laura Levine)

Buck was fond of saying that on "Wolves, Lower," they were aiming for "spooky gospel." While that term may be too vague to be useful, one has a sense of what he means. "Gothic" might be a slightly better term, and it could also apply to much of the record. It certainly applies to the record's cover, which features a photo of a gargoyle from Notre Dame in Paris, one of Europe's most splendid Gothic cathedrals.

"Ages of You" had undoubtedly been a serious contender for inclusion, and Buck later stated, admittedly without a lot of conviction, that he wished they'd used it. My guess is that the band first had doubts about "Ages of You" soon after the October '81 session. Probably when reviewing the tapes, they realized that four of the songs felt somehow linked, and that "Ages of You," good though it was, stood out too much. This, I think,

R.E.M.: <u>MURMUR</u>

is the real reason why they then opted to go back and cut "Wolves, Lower." Not because it was new and they wanted to try it out in the studio (in fact it was a good nine months old) but because—once they had a loose thematic concept for the record—it was felt that "Wolves" fitted it better than "Ages of You." Much as I like "Ages of You," I think it was the right decision. While *Chronic Town* does not by any means convey the full range of styles that R.E.M. were capable of, I think it's an extremely well-balanced record and one that flows perfectly from start to finish.

FOUR

REFLECTIONS ON MURMUR: THE ALBUM RECORDING SESSIONS

By the summer of '82, things were looking much better. R.E.M. finally had a record out that they felt proud of, and they were signed to a label they felt comfortable with. They had no money, of course, and were still touring the country in their old van, in which they continued to sleep on a regular basis. They toured extensively, playing in more places than just about any band before or since. Just as much as their records, it was that willingness to get out there and play, no matter how rotten the venue, that was the foundation of their ultimate success.

IRS, as noted, was less than happy with the production of *Chronic Town*. Their reservations were justified to some extent; the production lacked a certain polish and depth. IRS was unable to understand that the lack of production values didn't matter and that the music was more important than anything else. Despite the fact that the band spent considerable time that summer out on the West Coast getting to know the staff at IRS, there seems to have been a lack of communication. The first real manifestation of the problem came at the end of the year when it was time for the band to start recording an album.

An original proof sheet for the *Murmur* sleeve head shots. The "annotations" are the ones made by Stipe at the time.
(PHOTO BY SANDRA LEE-PHIPPS)

Song recorded: Catapult

IRS's reservations about *Chronic Town* extended beyond the production itself—it seems they were also unhappy with its producer and the studio in which it was made. Easter claims that he wasn't surprised. After all, he was completely unknown to the company and was working out of his parents' garage: "No doubt IRS thought I was some Southern good buddy sound man friend of [the band] who's not qualified to make a real record for a real record company."

In consequence, IRS persuaded the band to do a test recording in a "real" 24-track studio, with a different producer. The man they chose was Stephen Hague, who would later work with the Human League, Orchestral Manoeuvres in the Dark, and New Order. Although his more famous work came later, Hague was already a producer noted for his love of synthesizers and click tracks, which was a million miles from the music of R.E.M.

How much the band were coerced into working with Hague is open to question. Jay Boberg claims that it was "just an idea" and denies any bias against Easter, citing the fact that he'd already started talking to Easter about signing Easter's own band, Let's Active. Even Peter Buck has said that it was a case of, "OK, we'll try it"—while at the same time stressing that they'd much rather continue working with Easter.

Whatever the circumstances, Hague and R.E.M. was not a marriage made in heaven. Somehow, he got the band to do nearly fifty takes of "Catapult," which he later took apart and reassembled, using, for instance, the bridge from one take and the chorus from another. Bill Berry suffered more directly than the others. Hague set up a click track to "help you keep time"—a most dispiriting thing for a drummer to hear, especially one as good as Berry. He also told Berry to hit the drums harder. Berry, no mean thumper to begin with, hit them harder. Yet still the producer said, "Harder," and so on, ad infinitum. By the end of the session, Berry was crazed and demoralized, and the others weren't in much better shape. Hague returned to Boston and remixed the tapes. In due course, the band received the finished cut, which, by now, was swamped with synthesizers. They were angry and embarrassed and vowed that no one would ever hear the tape. And assuming it still exists, no one outside the immediate circle ever has.

More surprisingly, perhaps, IRS didn't like it much either and were persuaded by the band to give Easter a chance. The irony is that if Hague's track had been only a little less awful, the band would have found IRS a lot more intransigent. As it was, IRS still wasn't prepared to give Mitch the final go ahead to do a complete album. He too had to make a test recording of one song.

Song recorded: "Pilgrimage" (used on *Murmur*)

Reflection Studios, Charlotte, NC, December 1982 or Early January 1983

For his "test," Easter selected Reflection, a 24-track studio in nearby Charlotte, used primarily for gospel recordings. Partly because he was unfamiliar with the board, and partly because he didn't want to come on like a hot-shot producer, he asked Don Dixon, an old friend, to help.

Dixon is an interesting guy. Some five years older than Mitch, he'd been around the Winston-Salem scene for years. Easter described him as "this real dramatic guy with big hippy hair." He'd been a longstanding member of Arrogance, a North Carolina rock band that had lasted nearly 15 years and were a local institution. They cut several albums that hadn't gone anywhere, so in order to supplement his income Dixon taught himself to be a studio engineer. In fact, nearly seven years earlier he'd helped engineer a record by the Sneakers, the band that featured Easter and other Winston-Salemites.

Dixon assisted Mitch, uncredited, with the mixing of "Wolves, Lower." He had seen R.E.M. live and was so blown away that he more or less insisted on working with Mitch. Peter Buck later said of him: "He hates the music business and hates it when bands sound real professional. He knows how to get that real commercial sound . . . so he tries to trash up the recording process."

Dixon and Easter were exactly what the band needed, especially after their experience with Hague. Bill Berry, in particular, was still traumatized by the Hague session. Easter and Dixon had to be consistently supportive throughout the Reflection studio session to convince him of his talent, and that he didn't need to play like an automaton or even aspire to it. In fact, the whole band needed redirection post-Hague. According to Mitch, "We kind of yelled at them not to go in there and make a demo, but to make a record and experiment like we used to. Once we got that out of the way, I thought it got going really good." Which was a smart

move. Cutting a record rather than a "demo" (assuming the finished track was to everyone's satisfaction) meant there would be one less track that they had to cut at the real album sessions.

Which is pretty much the way it went. They chose to record "Pilgrimage"; it was the first time they attempted this song in a studio. Although the arrangement was fundamentally the same as the live one, the way it sounded was radically different and set the tone for the rest of the album. What they achieved was a dense layering, using multiple guitar tracks—some electric, some acoustic—and multiple vocal tracks. As Stipe later recalled: "We layered thousands of vocals on it to make it sound like a Gregorian chant. They're still there, way buried." Also, the studio's 24-track board meant that everything had a richer, fuller sound, certainly in comparison with *Chronic Town*.

With the test track completed, the band waited for IRS's response. When it came, it sadly wasn't particularly favorable, even if they did prefer it to Hague's track. At this point the band really began to wonder about IRS. When they signed with IRS, the band were virtually guaranteed artistic freedom, and certainly there was to be no pressure to come up with a hit single. That changed when IRS label-mates, the Go-Go's, had a hit and suddenly the company was down on R.E.M. to get one as well. The band more or less ignored the pressure, but IRS's cool reaction to "Pilgrimage" was part of the same attitude. This time the band refused to bow to pressure and told the label that they were happy with Easter and Dixon and proposed to make the album with them. The company capitulated, but the pressure didn't quite end there. On the first day of the full album sessions, Jay Boberg came down to the studio to lay it on the line. This time it was the producers who were told to deliver a hit. They too chose to ignore him. Effectively, though, from the moment that IRS agreed to the band's demand that they should continue with Mitch, R.E.M. were on their own.

Reflection was booked and the band was given a $15,000 budget, Easter and Dixon sharing a princely $2,000 advance for their services. At this juncture none of them were getting rich. As Buck told *Contrast* in 1986,

> When we were doing *Murmur* we were completely and utterly broke. We would pool like $2 and buy a quart of beer and split it. One night we were in a hotel and Bill was sitting in the lobby, whistling through his clasped hands when someone came up to him and said, "Hey, you can do that. We're shooting a Dodge commercial and we can't find anyone to do that. We'll give you $25 to do that." It was the 1983 Dodge commercial where the music was just like The Good, the Bad and the Ugly. So Bill went in and did it. He came out with twenty-five bucks, and we all go: "liquor store run!" That was the first outside session that anyone did from R.E.M.

Songs recorded: "Radio Free Europe," "Laughing," "Talk About the Passion," "Moral Kiosk," "Perfect Circle," "Catapult," "9-9," "Shaking Through," "We Walk," and "West of the Fields" (all of these tracks appear on the finished album). Outtakes: "Romance," "Ages of You." Live to two-track: "That Beat," "All the Right Friends," "Tighten Up," "There She Goes Again," "Moon River," "Pretty Persuasion." Plus remixing and overdubbing on "Sitting Still" (appears on the album).

Reflection Studios, Charlotte, NC, January 20–February 23, 1983 (approx. 16 days total)

Although the role of *Murmur*'s producers was vital, it would seem that the band, especially Buck, had a pretty clear idea of what they wanted, even if they didn't know how to achieve it. As Buck later recalled, "I knew which songs were going to be on the record and had a good idea of what order they were going to be in. I had pretty much in mind what I wanted: an acoustic guitar, a load of electric guitars, a soft electric guitar, and a 12-string, and Mitch and Don would find ways to make it all sound interesting. We [the band] didn't know enough to know what we were doing. The arrangement ideas were all ours, then Mitch would say: 'Why don't you record a 12-string like this and mike the strings, as opposed to miking the amp?' A lot of what kind of makes that album sound the way it does was making all the weird instrumental ideas we had work together."

The other area where the band needed rehabilitation following their experience with Hague was the use of any modern technology that might have given R.E.M. anything approaching a hi-tech sound. "Real" instruments of any sort were okay, which in R.E.M.'s case meant guitars, pianos (most notably on "Shaking Through" and "Perfect Circle"), and an organ, which Mike Mills played on "West of the Fields." However, the band would panic any time the producers suggested anything that smacked of a synthesizer or other electronic device. But, as Mitch wryly put it: "They didn't know that Don and I have impeccable taste."

As well as knowing which songs they wanted on the record, the band also came up with a role model for the album. As Buck told *Trouser Press* in 1983, "The idea was to make a strong record with no filler, like *Aftermath* by the Stones, where every song is different, but it sounds like a group effort."

In fact, although it sounds like a group effort, *Murmur* was actually less so than their earlier recordings. The normal format on *Murmur* was for the whole band to cut the basic track for a song, after which the overdubs were usually completed with just one of them working alone with the producers. The others, meanwhile, would be off playing pool, watching TV, or whatever. Easter later claimed that he missed the intensity of the Drive-In sessions but felt that the changes were inevitable, bearing in mind how much longer they were spending on the recordings. What they did on *Murmur*, however, although pretty much for the last time, was to work on one—or at most two—songs at a time, and finish them before moving on to a new one.

As noted, Buck claimed that he knew what songs they were going to include before they went into the studio. This sounds like it had required a lot of forethought, but, even though they'd written an impressive number of excellent songs over the previous two-and-a-half years, the choices were limited. In fact, if you eliminate the songs they actually recorded during the main *Murmur* sessions, along with the seven already released, plus the two songs, "Seven Chinese Brothers" and "Pretty Persuasion," that they claimed were not really finished, there wasn't much left to choose from. To my mind there were only three other real contenders: "Just a Touch," "Windout," and "Rockville." I suspect the first two were excluded because they were too like the explosive up-tempo rockers already slated for the album, and "Rockville," was probably deemed too bright and happy and would, thus, never have fitted in with the overall feel of *Murmur*.

To some extent this lack of material explains the reappearance on the album of the two Hib-Tone songs, "Radio Free Europe" and "Sitting Still." Justifying their presence on *Murmur* was, to a certain extent, fairly easy. Although the Hib-Tone single had been well reviewed, its low print run and poor distribution meant that relatively few people had heard it. And they are, after all, both great songs. There was, however, another reason for their inclusion on *Murmur*, at least in the case of one of them. It seems that IRS had pretty much insisted that the band rerelease "Radio Free Europe" at the earliest opportunity. It has even been suggested that it was a stipulation written into the deal. Whether or not the band were contractually obligated is open to question, but it's certainly true that Jay Boberg pushed the band to pay off Hibbert, leaving the way open for them to reuse the songs. Aside from the possibility (indeed probability) that Boberg simply loved the song, one can only assume that IRS thought that it was the one most likely to be a hit. If R.E.M. came up with something else, fine, but this way IRS was hedging their bets. This is only speculation, but it is supported by the fact that "Radio Free Europe" was the first R.E.M. single released by IRS. To be fair to Boberg, he genuinely liked the band and could see beyond their potential, such as it was, to be hit makers. Evidently, the only reason "9-9" ended up on *Murmur* was because Boberg loved it and specifically asked them to record it. This impressed them because all parties knew "9-9" was far too off-beat to be a single.

As far as I know, even if the band were obliged to reuse "Radio Free Europe," they did not actually have to rerecord it. But that's what they chose to do because they couldn't figure out exactly what was wrong with the original. Whether the new version is, indeed, better is itself a matter of controversy. It's slower than the Hib-Tone track and probably has greater clarity and depth, but it lacks the manic edge of the original. However, when compared to the cleaned-up version of the original that was used on *Eponymous*, it's a much tougher call.

Easter vaguely regrets that they couldn't have achieved a compromise between the two recordings. Buck is simply adamant that it was a mistake to have rerecorded the song at all, and he may be right. His argument is that it was an old song they'd played to death and, therefore, it was impossible to recapture the right feel. But his argument doesn't hold water. At least three other songs on *Murmur* were written around the same time as "Radio Free Europe," and three more were already nine months to a year old by the time the band went in to record the album. In fact, only two songs on *Murmur*, "We Walk" and "Talk About the Passion," were written after the completion of *Chronic Town*.

There is one further difference between the Hib-Tone and *Murmur* versions of "Radio Free Europe." Before the *Murmur* version actually starts, there's an odd little blast of what sounds like static or some other form of sonic distortion. According to Easter, "It's static from the console amplified a whole lot and gated to the bass guitar pattern from the 'raving station' part of the song. We felt that it was a kind of groovy, mysterious intro, and by keying the signal to turn off and on with the rhythm of the bass guitar, it was sort of subliminally related to the track." Got that?

Although the band had quite early on admitted that "Sitting Still," was the Hib-Tone recording, many writers continued to assume it was a new version. In truth, the *Murmur* version sounds different, but much of that was a result of Don and Mitch's excellent remix, which did include slowing the track down a little. However, Mike Mills also provided a new bass line that really strengthens the performance. Also, some of the background vocals were redone, which probably helped as well. Although it blends in with the new recordings, "Sitting Still" is certainly a simpler production than the rest of the album. It has no multitracked guitars, layered voices, or strange noises.

Easter and Dixon may have had trouble convincing the band to use new technology, but they had no trouble getting their okay to play on the record. Several of the tracks, notably "Laughing" and "Talk About the

Passion," feature one or both of the producers on acoustic guitar. In fact, according to Easter, "A whole bunch of us played acoustic guitars on that ["Laughing"]. We did this sort of protest sit-in thing with four people on acoustic guitar. It was me, Don Dixon, Pete Buck, and Mike Mills. Then we tracked it again, so there are eight acoustic guitars on it." Also, on "Perfect Circle" Dixon played bass and Easter plays electric guitar (inserted as a backward tape). Not surprisingly, Easter later described the sessions as predominantly "ego-free."

The producers weren't the only non-R.E.M. musicians on the record. "Talk About the Passion" actually features a guest cellist. As Buck told me in 1983, "We hired this lady from the symphony orchestra. We paid her 25 dollars. We told her roughly what we wanted, and she was dumbfounded that we weren't going to give her a score. But she was great in the end."

Overall, *Murmur* is full of little innovations and additions that enhanced the final record. On "Moral Kiosk," for example, rather than use a sampler, the band banged on bits of wood. The resulting noise was recorded with a lot of compression to get the desired percussive sound.

The most famous added effects, however, are on "We Walk." It was a problematic song to start with, particularly the drum pattern, which had to be rock steady. With shades of Stephen Hague hovering, Berry played the basic lick, which was recorded and then looped by Easter, and that's what they used. Even then, it wasn't quite right, so they hit on the solution of recording a pool game taking place in the rec room beneath the studio. They took the recording of the balls colliding, slowed it down, and added it to the track of "We Walk." No one was quite sure why, but it worked, with several of the crashes resounding, quite fortuitously, at exactly the right moments. The balls sound either like depth charges or thunder, depending on your point of view.

On "9-9" the producers themselves adopted a different approach. As Easter later explained: "We kind of mixed it in a different way. We ran the whole song back into the studio through some speakers and re-miked it to make it sound kind of different." The vocals in "9-9" also deserve a special mention because they were recorded so as to be almost, but not quite, indecipherable. Which is not to say that the other vocals on the album were clear as a bell, of course, just that they weren't deliberately recorded that way.

Don Dixon recalls: "At the time, Michael was particularly self-conscious about the lyrics. He would pull out a matchbook that would have something on it, and that's what he was taking his words from. It wasn't like he was organized. We protected Michael a lot in terms of allowing him to feel completely free in the studio. We gave him his own space that no one could see in[to]. He could turn the lights on and off, he could lay down on the floor and sing if he wanted to. He could do anything he wanted to, and that probably gave him a certain freedom."

By and large, the sessions for *Murmur* went really well, and both the band and the producers were delighted with the results. To round off the proceedings, they held an impromptu extra session, recording six songs live, direct to two-track. None of the two-track recordings were taken very seriously, although all but one, "That Beat," have ended up on official or, at least, semi-official releases. Three of the six are originals: "Pretty Persuasion," "All the Right Friends," and the aforementioned "That Beat." The latter two songs date from the band's formative period and are less-than-riveting, but it's good to have even these primitive versions. "Pretty Persuasion" is the most interesting of the three. It's obvious that the final arrangement was in place, but Michael had yet to be satisfied with the lyrics—the reason, one assumes, that the song was not recorded during the main *Murmur* sessions. They did, of course, record a proper version of it for *Reckoning*.

The three covers show exactly how eclectic, not to say eccentric, the band could be. "There She Goes Again," the Velvet Underground song, is almost very good. It's marred only by Stipe's missing a verse and screwing up the ending. Buck, who plays acoustic guitar on the track alongside Easter, has fond memories of having to step up to the mike to take his solo: "Just like Bill Monroe." Although the track was never seriously considered for inclusion on the album, they did toy with the idea of putting it on the cassette version as a bonus track. The song was finally dropped, but not before a whole batch of inserts were printed listing the track. Despite its nonappearance on the tape, the original cassette with the incorrect insert is considered a major R.E.M. collectors' item.

By contrast, the version of Archie Bell and the Drells classic "Tighten Up" is hilarious. Despite the title, the arrangement is anything but tight, but it does feature Mitch Easter taking a xylophone solo, which is worth the price of admission on its own.

The last cover is "Moon River," the Henry Mancini and Johnny Mercer theme from *Breakfast at Tiffany's*, one of Stipe's favorite songs from his childhood. In concert it was usually sung a cappella by Stipe, Mills, and Berry. Here, though, Stipe performs it solo, with tasteful piano accompaniment from Mills.

As noted, five of the six live to two-track songs have been released officially—sort of. "There She Goes Again" was issued with the band's blessing as a B-side and, later, on *Dead Letter Office*. The other four were issued as bonus tracks on the early '90s European CD reissues of *Reckoning* ("Pretty Persuasion," "Moon River," and "Tighten Up") and *Dead Letter Office* ("All the Right Friends"). The band did not sanction any of the bonus cuts on the albums that IRS reissued after they left the label. R.E.M. claim that several of the tracks, though not necessarily the five mentioned above, were taken off bootlegs and that IRS had no legal right to issue them. The label has vigorously insisted that all of the tracks were taken from master tapes deposited with the company by the band and, as a result, they had every right to release them.

It's worth noting that the European CD of *Murmur* also contains bonus tracks, but nothing previously unreleased. For the record they are: "There She Goes Again" (again) plus vintage live versions of "9-9," and "Gardening at Night," both recorded at the Paradise, in Boston, on July 13, 1983; and "Catapult" from the Music Hall, Seattle, Washington, June 27, 1984. All three of the live tracks had previously appeared on single B-sides.

After the *Murmur* sessions were finished, the only thing left to do was the mixing. The mix was definitely in keeping with the way the tracks had been produced. As Buck later recalled: "It sounds like someone who never mixed a record mixed the record. [But] we worked with two pro mixers, we knew what we were doing . . . we fought over mixes, we remixed stuff, we worked really hard to get it just like that." He also told the *NME* in 1993, when comparing *Murmur* to the band's 1988 album, *Green*: "*Murmur* is more about warmth and things being together. It's not the kind of record where you sit and admire the pristine clarity of the separation. I mean, there's about twenty acoustic guitars on some tracks. It's supposed to be a mush. We worked really hard to get it to be a mush." For that reason Buck prefers the original vinyl version of the record, feeling that the CD picks out a lot of sounds that were deliberately buried deep in the mix.

In the end, the only real sour note over *Murmur* was "Catapult." The band, especially Buck, later disowned the mix. Easter, on the other hand, thinks it's fine and concludes that the band had been so screwed up by Hague that they came to loathe the song. Consequently, no mix would have satisfied them.

That reservation aside, the band were excited by the results. Buck later remarked:

I remember thinking, "God, I can't wait until everyone hears this." Because it was different. It didn't sound like our other records, it didn't sound like us live, and it didn't sound like anything else that was coming out. It was the first time I thought all the songs were really strong, some of them were so on the money, I was real happy. I didn't know if anyone else was gonna like it. In fact we played it for our friends, and they were all saying "God, that's weird, it doesn't sound like you at all."

R.E.M. marvel at the overnight appearance of the dreaded kudzu. An outtake from the *Murmur* cover session.
(Photo by Sandra Lee-Phipps)

He needn't have worried.

Murmur was released in the United States on April 13, 1983, housed in one of the more unusual and least commercial jackets ever to grace a rock album. The sepia front cover photo looks like a cross between a Gothic hayfield and the Addams Family's backyard. In fact, it's a landscape covered in kudzu, a strange Japanese vine that some bright individual imported into Georgia. It grows so fast that if you turn your back on it, before you know what's happened, it will engulf trees, fields, houses, and whole towns. Well, maybe not whole towns—but its rapid spread has caused alarm all over the state.

It's been suggested that if the cover of *Chronic Town* was Gothic, then the cover of *Murmur* is, most assuredly, southern Gothic. This brings up the whole nature of the band in relation to the South. For the press, the relative novelty of R.E.M.'s southern affiliations was too good to ignore. Pretty soon they found themselves defending the South, or at least the "New South," at the same time they dropped the names of writers like Flannery O'Connor and Carson McCullers, whose work began to be compared with R.E.M. or, rather, vice versa. The band also brought up southern characters, like the Reverend Howard Finster and his peace garden. His folk artwork would grace R.E.M.'s second album, *Reckoning*.

Of course, the full flowering of R.E.M.'s or, more specifically, Stipe's love of southern culture, would not happen until their third album, *Fables of the Reconstruction*. Nonetheless, there are those who would argue that it was there from the start, manifested primarily in the *Murmur* cover, but also, albeit obliquely, in some of the lyrics or the atmosphere created by the songs. John Seavwright, a friend of the band, described north Georgia to *Vox* in 1993: "It's sunny here, but there's a darkness and decay as well. There's a constant reminder of mortality." Seavwright's statement certainly brings to mind some of the lyrics on *Chronic Town* and, in some ways, the overall atmosphere of *Murmur*. It also conjures up the feel of another, more recent work about Georgia, albeit Savannah rather than Athens, *Midnight in the Garden of Good and Evil*.

Just how southern R.E.M. really are, as individuals, is open to question. In *Talk About the Passion*, the oral history of the band, Georgia native Sean Bourne expressed his reservations on the subject:

They spoke about the south the way people who are in awe of it speak about the south. It was kind of like they read Flannery O'Connor and said, "This is too weird." Me being from the south and knowing people like Flannery O'Connor's characters—it's no big deal. It's still fascinating and wonderful, but it's not with a sense of awe I speak about them. I don't think R.E.M. were about the south as much as they were intrigued by it: "Hey look at this, look at this weird guy here."

Balanced against that take on R.E.M. is the view of a fellow southern musician, Gil Ray, "I don't think unless you're from the South, you can really understand their connection to the South completely. Seeing kudzu on the album cover . . . I could relate."

The rear cover photo on *Murmur* looks not so much southern as just plain odd, like a close-up of something a prisoner would make out of match sticks. It's really a wooden train trestle located just outside of Athens. Superimposed over the photo are individual portrait shots of each of the band members. They all look extremely seedy, and the photos are not captioned.

The back of the sleeve also contains a track list, typed by Stipe. It bears no relation to the running order on the record, and the letters of "Moral Kiosk" run vertically down through the other titles.

The inner sleeve is almost as much fun as the outer one. In large white smudgy type (probably Stipe's own machine again), we are offered a certain amount of information relating to the album: when and where it was recorded; the producers; the jacket artists' names; and the band members' names (well, first names anyway), but no instrument designations. The other side contains another track listing, in order this time.

What the album does not contain is a lyric sheet. As Buck told *Creem* in 1986,

The best thing that Michael did—they were insisting on a lyric sheet for *Murmur*. So Michael took—we wrote about twenty songs in the space of a year that were gonna be on *Murmur*, ended up playing fifteen—he took all his favorite phrases from all of these songs, some that weren't on the record, some that were deleted from the songs. He arranged them as a short story and gave them one paragraph. It almost made sense. And they said: "Well I guess we won't put out a lyric sheet this time." We don't get much pressure from them now.

Stipe summed up his own view of lyric sheets, in typically colorful style, to *Alternative America*, shortly after *Chronic Town* was released. It was one of the first times the issue had been seriously raised. Stipe noted,

> Frankly, I think lyric sheets are ridiculous. Some horrible thing happened when The Beatles put out their white album. I think that was the first record to ever have a lyric sheet [sic]. To take something like lyrics and remove them from a song is like taking someone's liver out of their body and putting it on a table and asking it to work. You take it out of context, and it really doesn't make any sense. To contradict that, we're probably going to have a lyric sheet to the album [*Murmur*]. But it could very easily be in Braille.

Sure.

One thing the front sleeve of *Murmur* does have, fortunately, is the name of the band and the title of the album. What's the significance of the album's name? That was one of the most frequently asked questions after it was released, right up there with what do the letters R.E.M. stand for. The answer to that one depended on the mood of the band member being asked: "Rhinos, Elephants, and Mooses" was one response; "Rear End Men" was Buck's favorite if he was fed up and wanted the interviewer to move on. It actually stands, of course, for "Rapid Eye Movement," but they never used the spelled-out form. In fact, virtually their first booking contract specified that the name should not be spelled out on advertising for shows.

Stipe, at least, was usually more serious when it came to *Murmur*. He told several interviewers that it was one of the six, sometimes seven, easiest words to say in the English language: "I think it comes right after 'mama,' which is probably why it was picked. It's got nice implications, I guess." It certainly does. The dictionary defines it as "a low indistinct but often continuous sound" and "a soft or gentle utterance." Both of those relate directly to the album's music and, of course, as several critics were quick to point out, Stipe's singing style.

The whole band thought *Murmur* was a good record, but none of them expected the critical acclaim. Apart from the occasional jibe about Stipe's vocals, the reviews were almost unanimously favorable, frequently bordering on the ecstatic. Top of the list was a four-star review in *Rolling Stone*, after which it was named album of the year in their critics poll, above Michael Jackson's *Thriller*. The same poll also placed R.E.M. as "Best New Band" and third, after U2 and Police, in the general "Band of the Year" listing. It was an extraordinary reaction. Virtually every type of newspaper and magazine, from the highbrow (*New York Times*) to the smallest fanzine (*Trouser Press*) to the trades (*Billboard*) loved the record.

It's hard to pin down exactly why it was so beloved. It is a great record, but that's never stopped critics panning an album. Timing, of course, is everything. The ghost of disco still lingered and, in the United States at least, the most popular bands were British synth-pop groups, like Haircut 100 and Soft Cell, whose music was little more than a studio confection for young teenagers. In R.E.M., the critics found a band clearly comprised of grown-up real musicians, whose music, while decidedly edgy and gritty, was melodic and potentially commercial. For many critics, particularly those over thirty not wanting to give up their youth, it was a combination made in heaven.

To some extent, and not really surprisingly, the album sales, while very good for a first album, did not quite match the reviews. Whereas *Thriller* went straight to number one and stayed there, *Murmur* peaked at number 36 on the *Billboard* chart, where it remained for three weeks.

That it did *that* well was a result of two factors, aside from the reviews. The first was R.E.M.'s continued willingness to go out and play anywhere, night after night. The second factor was college radio, which evolved a symbiotic relationship with R.E.M., the one's success feeding off the other. Buck told a radio interviewer in early 1983: "College radio is behind us. I don't expect to be on AM radio. College radio means that we can play pretty much anywhere in the country and draw a fairly wide audience of discriminating people, rather than a bunch of lumpheads who heard us on an AM station."

Mike Mills was even more outspoken when he told *Zigzag* in 1984:

College radio is great. We think it has probably been the savior of American radio. They started [by] playing the music that the Top 40 and AOR stations wouldn't play, though some enterprising stations, such as KNAC, in Los Angeles, and WBRU in Providence, Rhode Island, have taken on a college-style musical format, and they're great, too.

R.E.M. didn't single-handedly create college radio, nor were the college stations solely responsible for R.E.M.'s success. Nonetheless, the band's importance for the stations cannot be underestimated. As IRS promo man Keith Altomare told author Denise Sullivan:

What we did with them at IRS was Miles Copeland's philosophy. He and Michael Plen [then head of radio promotion at IRS] decided college radio was the way to build them. . . . Because of R.E.M., college radio started to take other bands close to its heart and after *Murmur,* other bands were out there competing for the same slot.

Regarding the critical reaction to *Murmur*, it's worth pointing out that not everybody got it. Take the example of Bill Bailey, then a DJ at WLKS in Atlanta. In early 1984 he was quoted as saying that R.E.M. needed to become "a little more commercial to get as big as, say, Journey. They need to produce the words better, although the production isn't that far from the mainstream. The more commercial the sound, the more mass appeal it will have."

Even stronger was the reaction of Robert Christgau, music editor at the *Village Voice*, who, in fact, had been an early champion of the band. Noting that R.E.M. had done incredibly well in his annual critics poll, he commented in relation to *Murmur*: "The more I listen to it, the less I like it. I find it shallow, really shallow. They're a critic's band. They're savvy, avant-garde, and the music's full of hooks. If I sound slightly cynical about them, it's because I am." Christgau's own choice for album of the year? Avant-garde jazz guitarist James Blood Ulmer's *Odyssey*. Well, *Odyssey's* certainly not full of hooks, that's for sure.

Whether *Murmur* is R.E.M.'s best album is impossible to gauge. It remains my favorite, an opinion not shared by the band, but then it would be odd if they did. I think it's held up incredibly well and still bears repeated listening, thanks in part to the production, which enables the listener to find new things in it after all this time.

I'll leave the last word to *Murmur*'s producer, Mitch Easter: "I thought that the final result was really cool and that it still sounds odd and distinctive. I was pleased with it, although when we got finished, I had no idea if it was the right thing or not." It was.

Buck tries to convince an arena full of Police fans that R.E.M. are really one of the hottest live bands in the country. JFK Stadium, Philadelphia, August 1983.
(PHOTO BY LAURA LEVINE)

R.E.M.: <u>MURMUR</u>

REVIEWS

R.E.M.'S Record "Murmur" Is an Adventurous Experiment
By J. Eddy Ellison
Classic Scene, April 1983

R.E.M., Athens' most popular band, is well on its way to national success with the release of their first I.R.S. Records album, "Murmur." This is an excellent product that is surprisingly bold as it does not attempt to recapture the R.E.M. live sound.

R.E.M. have made their reputation as a major national rock act through their constant touring—presenting a hard charging, rock 'n' roll show second to none. That they would not attempt the probably impossible job of re-creating this show is a credit to their artistic integrity and a perhaps unplanned but nonetheless shrewd marketing strategy.

R.E.M., along with the B-52's and Pylon, have been burdened by the national media as having "the Athens Sound." This meaningless term apparently tries to unite these three disparate groups simply because of their intense danceability.

R.E.M. definitely shares a common bond with the Bees and Pylon in this respect, and they could rightfully be called the Kings of Athens dance bands.

It was pretty much assumed that when R.E.M. caught up with the Bees and Pylon they would similarly attempt to create their dance-party onto vinyl.

Forget it kids. This ain't no party.

"Murmur" presents twelve tunes which slip the dance rhythm into the background, slow up the tempo and push up the melody and vocals.

This bears no resemblance to the sound which attracts 1200 Athenians to each R.E.M. show.

For one thing, the vocals are treated very well here. Michael Stipe does an outstanding job of projecting his somewhat obtuse lyrics with varying tones and inflections. A live rock format just can't bring this out.

The absolute standout attraction on this disc, though, is Pete Bucks' beautifully melodic guitar. A self-described "three-chord wonder," old Pete's Rickey shimmers and rings, producing a sound very similar to the late sixties group, the Byrds.

What sets Pete's sound apart from that of past melody meisters is the use of studio effects which serve to widen the tonal range without seeming murky. A credit to the pure and easy production of Mr. Mitch Easter.

Side One leads off with "Radio Free Europe," which was the A side of their first release in 1981. This version has been remixed due to a bad mastering job on the first single (which nonetheless was dubbed independent single of the year by the *Village Voice*'s Robert Christgau). The most FM rock-oriented of all R.E.M. songs, this one leaves me a bit dry but is intensely catchy. Please replace Loverboy, etc., with this. I won't mind.

"Pilgrimage" is the first indication of what this record is about. Though as compelling as the live version, it is slower and utilizes subtle vocal phrasings. Sometimes you can tell what is being said and sometimes you can't. The effect is neat and a little spooky. The words go from a dramatic crescendo to a whisper to conversational tone. All the while the music weaves itself around the plot. I like it.

"Laughing," "Talk About the Passion," and "Moral Kiosk" are all aural vignettes reflecting some aspect of Michael Stipe's world view. Each poem-song is an emotional statement. That half the lyrics are indecipherable is unimportant. The feeling is there, and that is enough. I think that if we did have all the lyrics at our disposal it would take away all the fun and mystique from these tunes.

"Perfect Circle" is the perfect song for this album. It is a dreamy, classical piece built around a repeating piano riff. It is totally unlike anything R.E.M. have ever attempted live and thus is a most fitting tune for this album. This is my favorite song on "Murmur."

Even though this is a guitar/vocal-oriented album, Bill Berry's drumming and Mike Mills' bass are excellent throughout. Though subdued, each has a precision and strength upon which the fragility of the song structure relies.

Side two starts with "Catapult." I have yet to come across anyone who knew what Michael was saying in this tune. I thought it was "Had a cold," and some think it was "Got to go." A song about adolescence which is typically oblique but, once again, the sound's the thing. I think Michael once said that it was the sound of the words rather than their meaning that is important. This is not a sing-along group.

"Sitting Still," the B-side of "Radio Free Europe," is much cleaner sounding than the original. I would rather have seen two unreleased songs such as "Pretty Persuasion" than these two, but it was probably a good marketing decision.

"9-9." I don't know what this is about but the guitar is very innovative in the overdubbing department. "Shaking Through" is the greatest departure from its live counterpart than any other tune on "Murmur." The thing to remember here, is that R.E.M. live relies heavily on visuals. A record that tried to capture the live sound without Stipe's "puppet with one foot nailed to the floor" writhing and Buck's Keith Richardian strut would probably be a disappointment.

"We Walk" is the second best tune on the album for the same reason as "Perfect Circle." This sounds like an ode to Michael's sister Lynda. In fact, the lilting flow and the subject matter of this tune seems like something Lynda herself might have written for her group, Oh-Ok.

As with all of Michael's lyrics, I think personal interpretations of the subject matter are more fun than actually knowing what they're about. I hope Michael does not bow under pressure to include lyric sheets in future discs. Maybe a book of poems would be nice.

"Murmur" is wrapped up by the anthematic "West of the Fields." This song does for "Murmur" what "Carnival of Sorts (Boxcars)" did for their "Chronic Town" EP, provide a rousing, charged up capstone to the whole affair. While not as intense as "Carnival" (nothing on this record approaches that energy level), "Fields" is still similarly uplifting and is the closest to the R.E.M. live sound of the twelve tunes.

"Murmur" is a bold and immensely likeable experiment from four guys that got their start playing at Kathleen O'Brien's birthday party at the church on Oconee Street. Next time around though, I would like to see some of their oldies, like "Can't Control Myself" and "Permanent Vacation," committed to vinyl.

You've done your art, guys, now let's have some fun!

"Murmur," R.E.M.
By Jonathan Gregg
Record, July 1983

R.E.M.'s is music of movement and portent, driven with vague obsession and as American as tumbleweeds and Manifest Destiny. Last year, this Athens, Georgia, band's debut EP, *Chronic Town,* blew in across a wasteland of domestic music and announced the quartet's arrival in no uncertain terms. Songs such as "Carnival of Sorts (Boxcars)," "1,000,000," and "Wolves, Lower" shackled mystery and melody to a propulsive, lean rhythm. Framed by the brittle filigree of Peter Buck's guitar, sinewy bass lines and slap-in-the-face drums, lead singer Michael Stipe's gravelly baritone growled mournful melodies from the underground, then rose triumphantly for climactic choruses, at once stirring and incomprehensible, like Mass sung in Latin.

This music has a center which is difficult to contemplate directly. Key phrases are either deliberately slurred or jumbled in the mix, while whole verses are often buried under the instrumental work: their meaning surfaces intermittently like fragments of a conversation overheard during a fitful sleep on a noisy train. Bolstered by Mitch Easter's discreet production, the band's unadorned '60s pop instrumental sound juxtaposed with Stipe's world-weary vocals—all supporting a host of first-rate songs—results in a splendid little film noir of an album, austere but rich in implication. In short, *Murmur* delivers on both the promise and the premise of *Chronic Town.*

Once again these are songs of movement and destiny, signified by titles on the order of "Pilgrimage," "We Walk," and "Catapult." Be it in the garbled rallying cry of war ("Radio Free Europe") or the tremors of new love ("Shaking Through"), the performances are imbued with the spirit of breakthrough and urgency. Though distinctly less bluesy than the Rolling Stones, the throbbing beat and rich chordal resolutions of "Moral Kiosk" and "Catapult" recall "Street Fighting Man" and "She's So Cold"; "9 to 9" captures the controlled chaos of "Have You Seen Your Mother, Baby?"; "Laughing," "Sitting Still" and "Shaking Through" are in the classic

American folk-rock vein of the Byrds; on "Perfect Circle" Stipe echoes Jim Morrison's vocal style. But these are only clues, not the key to the mystery of *Murmur*.

R.E.M.'s solid rock foundation is built on the driving pulse of its up-tempo songs; a twitchy, restless dance beat the band seem to have already claimed as its own. Witness how the clipped verses and chanting choruses of "Radio Free Europe" create the tension-and-release central to R.E.M.'s aesthetic. Rather than becoming an end in itself, Easter's symbiotic production heightens the dynamics, eschewing the New Romantics' wall of synthesized melancholy for more traditional and ambiguous sounds of alarm/celebration such as voices and bells.

Astride this lean mount, Stipe sings of the flawed indomitability of the human spirit, a theme summed up in the beautiful but disturbing "Pilgrimage," one of the finest forays into rock mysticism since the Doors' "Crystal Ship." Sings Stipe, as if reciting some pagan ritual: "Your luck / a two-headed cow . . . the pilgrimage has gained momentum / take your turn / take your fortune." Life may well be nothing more than another futile crusade, but there's dishonor in neglecting the battle.

When R.E.M.'s philosophical conceits meld with its musical vision the results are inspiring, if not totally comprehensible. R.E.M.'s message can be absorbed only obliquely and upon repeated listenings when the LP's vague center beckons us to return again and again to glean the truth from this near-inscrutable oracle. The salvation Stipe tells of is a very private one, in keeping with the notion that, ultimately, each one of us answers only to ourselves—redemption starts and must be pursued on a personal level, owing to the absence of universal directives on how to conduct our lives. It seems an important statement to make at a time when basic human values are under siege. Those who will stay with *Murmur* and ride out Stipe's elusive diction—Did he really say that? What did he really say?—will find the rewards manifold, the message instructive, the soul renewed.

Murmur
By Steve Pond
Rolling Stone, May 26, 1983

R.E.M.'s *Chronic Town* EP was one of last year's more invigorating, tuneful surprises: a record from an Athens, Georgia, band that cared not a whit for the fashionable quirks of that town's dance-rock outfits like the B-52's or Pylon. R.E.M. fashioned its own smart, propulsive sound out of bright pop melodies, a murky, neopsychedelic atmosphere and a host of late-Sixties pop-rock touches. The execution wasn't always up to the ideas—instrumentally, the band was still stumbling at times—but *Chronic Town* served notice that R.E.M. was an outfit to watch. *Murmur* is the record on which they trade that potential for results: an intelligent, enigmatic, deeply involving album, it reveals a depth and cohesiveness to R.E.M. that the EP could only suggest.

Murmur is a darker record than *Chronic Town*, but this band's darkness is shot through with flashes of bright light. Vocalist Michael Stipe's nasal snarl, Mike Mills' rumbling bass and Bill Berry's often sharp, slashing drums cast a cloudy, post punk aura that is lightened by Peter Buck's folk-flavored guitar playing. Many of the songs have vague, ominous settings, a trait that's becoming an R.E.M. trademark. But not only is there a sense of detachment on the record—these guys, as one song title says, "Talk about the Passion" more often then they experience it—but the tunes relentlessly resist easy scanning. There's no lyric sheet, Stipe slurs his lines and they even pick a typeface that's hard to read. But beyond that elusiveness is a restless, nervous record full of false starts and images of movement, pilgrimage, transit.

In the end, though, what they're saying is less fascinating than how they say it. And *Murmur*'s indelible appeal results from its less elusive charms: the alternately anthemic and elegiac choruses of such stubbornly rousing tunes as "Laughing" and "Sitting Still"; instrumental touches as apt as the stately, elegant piano in the ballad "Perfect Circle" and the shimmering folkish guitar in "Shaking Through"; above all, an original sound placed in the service of songs that matter. R.E.M. is clearly the important Athens band.

SELECTED DISCOGRAPHY

1. Sitting Still/Radio Free Europe/White Tornado
2. Sitting Still/Radio Free Europe/White Tornado/Radio Dub

(These are Easter mixes. "Radio Dub" never reissued legally.)

Radio Free Europe/Sitting Still, Hib-Tone HT-0001 7/81

(This is the Hibbert mix for "Radio Free Europe." Never reissued legally.)

Radio Free Europe (edit)/There She Goes Again IRS 9916 4/83

(A side is an edited version of the *Murmur* rerecording, B side is from the *Murmur* live to two-track session.)

***Chronic Town*, IRS SP 70502 8/82**

***Murmur*, IRS SP 70604 4/83**

***Reckoning* IRS SP 70044 4/84**

The original album contains three tracks, "Pretty Persuasion," "7 Chinese Bros.," and "(Don't Go Back To) Rockville," which were written during the *Murmur* period, but not properly recorded until the *Reckoning* sessions.

Dead Letter Office, IRS SP 70054 4/87

This album contains a number of tracks written or recorded during the *Murmur* period:

"There She Goes Again" (The *Murmur* live to two-track version.)
"Burning Down" (From the *Reckoning* live to two-track session.)
"White Tornado" (Recorded at Drive-In 4/81. This a remastered
  version of the one used on the 1980 promo cassette.)
"Windout" (One of two versions cut during the *Reckoning* live to
  two-track session.)

R.E.M.: <u>MURMUR</u>

"Ages of You" (In the notes to DLO, Buck claims this was recorded during the *Reckoning* sessions. However, it's almost certainly the version cut during the main *Murmur* sessions and then remixed the following year during the *Reckoning* sessions. It was remixed yet again in 1985, before it was finally issued.)

Eponymous IRS 6262 10/88

This compilation album contains three tracks of interest:

"Radio Free Europe." The sleeve note claims that this is the original Hib-Tone version. Strictly speaking, it isn't; rather it is the second of two mixes that Easter did at the time, and the one the band considered superior to Jonny Hibbert's mix. They were overruled by Hibbert who insisted that his mix should be the one released. This, then, is the only legitimate issue of Easter's second mix.

"Romance." This song was written in early 1981 and recorded during the main *Murmur* sessions. Not only was it left off that album, but it has never passed into circulation among collectors. This version of the song was recorded in 1986 for use on the soundtrack to the movie *Made In Heaven*. While fans would no doubt like to hear the original recording, it's very doubtful that it sounds much different from this one.

"Gardening at Night." This is the harsh vocal/acoustic guitar version from the Drive-In session October '81.

This series reissued the original albums with bonus tracks, several of which were previously unissued. It should be noted that the band did not sanction, or approve, the bonus cuts.

Reckoning, IRS (Europe) 0777 7 13159 23, 1994

"Tighten Up," "Moon River," and "Pretty Persuasion." (All recorded during the *Murmur* live to two-track session.)

"Windout (With friends)." (Recorded during the *Reckoning* live to two-track session.)

"White Tornado." (Recorded during the *Reckoning* live to two-track session. This was the fourth [!] recorded version of the tune.)

Dead Letter Office, IRS (Europe) 0777 7 13199 21, 1994

"All the Right Friends." (Recorded during the *Murmur* live to two-track session.)

"Gardening at Night." (Acoustic version recorded during the *Reckoning* live to two-track session. They also cut a new electric version at the same time that remains officially unreleased. It's never been clear why they should have wanted to cut one, let alone two, new versions of the song.)

Bootlegs

With the glaring exceptions of the February 1981 Bombay Studios session and the *Murmur* version of "Romance," virtually all of the unreleased or rare material recorded during the period is available on bootleg.

Unfortunately, the relevant tracks are scattered over a variety of records and are frequently mislabeled. It doesn't seem to have occurred to any of the bootleggers that you could fit all of the relevant tracks onto a double-CD set. Of course, even if it happens, the sound quality may well be horrendous.

Bearing in mind the difficulty involved in tracking down the bootlegs listed below, readers may find it easier to obtain tapes from other collectors, many of whom can now be located through the Internet.

For the sake of clarity, I have broken the listing down by the original sessions, indicating the bootlegs on which the relevant tracks may be found.

1. Wuxtry's Practice Session, July 6, 1980

The first available version of these tracks was *R.E.M. Slurred*, a cassette made up by Mark Methe, who had recorded the original session, which was given away to friends. It was a copy of *R.E.M. Slurred* that formed the basis of all the succeeding bootlegs.

All eight tracks from *R.E.M. Slurred* appear on *Early Movements* CD and *Chronic Murmurings* LP, and all except "Dangerous Times" appear on *Pretty Pictures* LP.

2. Drive-In Studios, April/May 1981

"Radio Free Europe." (The Hib-Tone single mix by Hibbert.) Appears on *Really Exciting Music* LP.

"Radio Free Dub" (Mitch Easter's dub mix of "Radio Free Europe.") Appears on *The Essential Demos. Vol. 1* CD, *Rave On* CD, and *Smokin' in the Boy's Room* LP.

3. Drive-In Studios, October 1981

"1,000,000." Mix two appears on *Chronic Murmurings* LP and *Really Exciting Music* LP.

"1,000,000." Mix three appears on *Early Movements* CD and *Chronic Murmurings* LP.

"Ages of You." Appears on *The Essential Demos. Vol. 1* CD, *Chronic Murmurings* LP, and *Really Exciting Music* LP.

"White Tornado." Appears on *Really Exciting Music* LP.

"Carnival of Sorts." The October 1981 version appears on *The Essential Demos. Vol. 1* CD, *Chronic Murmurings* LP, and *Really Exciting Music* LP.

"Shaking Through." Appears on *The Essential Demos. Vol. 1* CD.

"Jazz Lips." Appears on *Chestnut*, a 7" flexi single.

4. Drive-In Studios, January 1982

"Wolves, Lower." The January 1982 fast version of the track appears on *The Essential Demos. Vol. 1* CD, *Early Movements* CD, and *Chronic Murmurings* LP.

5. RCA Demos, NYC, February 1982

"Catapult." Appears on *The Essential Demos. Vol. 1* CD, *Early Movements* CD, *Chronic Murmurings* LP, and *Pretty Pictures* LP.

"Wolves, Lower." Appears on *Early Movements* CD, *Chronic Murmurings* LP, and *Pretty Pictures* LP.

"Laughing." Appears on *The Essential Demos. Vol. 1* CD, *Early Movements* CD, *Chronic Murmurings* LP, and *Pretty Pictures* LP.

"Romance." Appears on *The Essential Demos. Vol. 1* CD, *Early Movements* CD, *Chronic Murmurings* LP, and *Pretty Pictures* LP.

"Shaking Through." Appears on *Early Movements* CD, *Chronic Murmurings* LP, and *Pretty Pictures* LP.

"Carnival of Sorts." Appears on *Early Movements* CD, *Chronic Murmurings* LP, and *Pretty Pictures* LP.

"Stumble." Appears on *Early Movements* CD, *Chronic Murmurings* LP, and *Pretty Pictures* LP.

INDEX

Page numbers in italics indicate pages containing photos.

Buck, Peter (*cont.*)
    and Hib-Tone single, 84
    on "Jazz Lips," 1
    on lyric sheets, 113
    on mix of *Murmur*, 110
    on *Murmur* sessions, 86, 103, 104
    on origins of "Gardening at Night," 22
    on "Perfect Circle," 67–68
    on "Pretty Persuasion," 31
    on "Radio Free Europe," 38, 106
    on RCA sessions, 90–91
    on R.E.M.'s initials, 114
    on "Rockville," 13
    on "Romance," 39, 40
    as songwriter, 4, 7
    on songwriting, 1, 16, 18
    on "Stumble," 41
    on "Talk About the Passion," 72
    on "West of the Fields," 60
    on "Wolves, Lower," 96
"Burning Down," 26–27, 126
Burroughs, William, 18
Byrds, The, 21, 48

"Camera," 72
"Can't Control Myself," 122
"Carnival of Sorts (Box Cars)," 43–45, 92, 95, 121, 122
    Drive-In Studios (Oct. 1981), 85, 129
    Drive-In Studios (Jan. 27–28, 1982), 89
    RCA (Feb. 1982), 90, 130
Carnival of Souls, 44
"Catapult," 58–60
    in *Classic Scene* review, 121
    Drive-In Studios (Jan. 27–28, 1982), 89
    Music Hall (Seattle, WA, June 27, 1984), 110
    RCA (Feb. 1982), 90–92, 129
    in *Record* review, 122
    Reflection Studios (Jan. 20–23, 1983), 103, 110
    Unknown Studio (Atlanta, GA, Dec. 1982), 100–101
Chestnut (bootleg flexi single), 129
Chilton, Alex, 80
Christgau, Robert, 116, 120
Chronic Murmurings (bootleg LP), 128–130
Chronic Town EP, 6, 10, 19, 41, 57, 91, 94, 95, 97, 99–100, 102, 106, 114, 121–125
    cover art, 112

Church on Oconee Street. *See* Oconee Street Church
"Cinnamon Girl," 21
City Gardens (Trenton, NJ), 67
Classic Scene magazine, 119–122
college radio, 115–116
Copeland, Ian, 3, 8, 85, 92
Copeland, Miles, 3, 92, 94, 116
Copeland, Stewart, 3
Cousteau, Jacques, 9
Cramps, The, 85
Creem magazine, 113–114
"Crystal Ship," 123
"cut-up" method of writing, 18

"Dangerous Times," 9, 75
Dark Carnival (Ray Bradbury), 44
Dasht Hopes, 85, 90–94
David, Jacques Louis, 70
dB's, 80, 81, *83*
Dead Letter Office, 27, 29, 109, 126–127
Dead Letter Office (European CD), 110, 128
"Different Girl," 9, 75
discography, 125–130
Dixon, Don, 67, 101, 103, 104, 106–108
"(Don't Go Back to) Rockville." *See* "Rockville"
Doors, The, 123
Downs, Bertis, 5, 14, 28–29, *54*, 84
Drive-In Studios, 5, 6, 81–90, 95–97, *96*
Duke, Dory, 70

Early Movements (bootleg CD), 128–130
Easter, Mitch, 80, 81, 85–88, *96*, 104, 106, *107*, 108, 120, 122, 123
    band's first visit to, 5
    as guitarist, 67, 107
    and IRS Records, 100, 101, 103
    and *Murmur*, 92, 94, 110, 117
    on "9–9," 53, 89
    on "Perfect Circle," 66
    and "Pilgrimage," 101
    and "Radio Free Europe," 82, 84
    on "Romance," 40
    on "Shaking Through," 32
    on "Sitting Still," 34
    on "Stumble," 40
    on "Talk About the Passion," 72
    on "West of the Fields," 60
    on "White Tornado," 39
    on "Wolves, Lower," 95
    as xylophonist, 109
Ellison, J. Eddy, 119–122
Elysian Fields, 60, 62
End of the Road (John Barth), 49, 51